I0523723

Driving For

Phillip Aughey

Driving For

Phillip Aughey

BLACK COCKIE PRESS

Driving For

Published by Black Cockie Press

Copyright © Phillip Aughey 2024

The moral right of the author has been asserted

Cover design © Natalie Muller 2024

Distributed by IngramSpark

Printed by IngramSpark

ISBN: 978-0-6454896-9-9

Scott, part 1

The road headed north, away from Sydney. It was taking me away from the buildings that I saw as a cancer upon the earth. I wanted to see the earth again. It was taking me away from a gloomy winter where the cold accentuated my unhappy mood. Descending onto the bridge crossing the Hawkesbury River, the afternoon sun, of an early spring day, beamed gaily upon the shimmering water. An endless forest of gum trees lined the slopes into the large river. The expanse of water gave me a taste of space that I had been fantasising about. I could see nature at last.

It was taking me away from the confused behaviour of the many people who were always wanting for something. They were never happy, they were never at peace. Their views were restricted by the buildings. The wall on the other side of the street locked them into a very insular cocoon.

I found myself descending into the daily routine they all suffered from. I was becoming trapped again. I needed to escape and recognise this was not for me. I was looking for my peace of mind again.

It was not to be found on this busy expressway. The little metal boxes with motors filed around me as if to trap me in, again. They had no care for the other metal boxes. It did not register that inside that anonymous metallic cage was another soul. It was all about them and their wants.

I stayed in the slow lane. I was not in a hurry. I had the rest of my life ahead of me. Time was not an issue as it was to these rushing past me. I was free to do whatever I wished at any time. I liked it that way.

About the time when I'd had enough of the other box's impatience I noticed a sign heading off this freeway, pointing inland. I hoped it would take me away from the confusion and aggression of this current path.

The bypass bought me onto what was obviously a newer road. I could tell because the surface was much smoother. I crossed through a series of wooded sloping hills. The ever increasing wattle blossoms seemed to act as a forerunner to something glorious beyond these hills. Soon I could see that the horizon was going to open up to a more congenial expansive scene. I was impatient to see that.

The gum tree forests gave way to more open paddocks. Green fields occupied with livestock, started to fill the scene. The change was happening. I began to feel more relaxed.

Turn offs to other villages and towns adorned the way and I wondered about them. It was later in the afternoon and although the traffic heading my direction, west, was much less than the previous freeway heading north, the traffic heading east was quite pronounced. I wondered why?

Another turn off to another village and the road started to climb slowly. The forest, featuring a different species of gum trees and pines, enclosed the side of the roads, as if leading me onto a horizon beyond this hill. The path was obvious by the increasing number of metal boxes heading in the opposite direction.

The pinnacle of the hill was heralded by a service station on the left. I paid it little attention as I was in expectation of the view soon to be opened. The trees diminished and open paddocks enlightened the way to a vast horizon developing as the summit was reached.

The vastness of the opening blue sky was only matched by the beauty of the scene now displayed before me. Where the sky met the earth, to my left and to my right, there were hills. They were increasingly taller the further the distance to them. They headed northwest like parallel lines that did meet at the horizon. They were the sentinels to what was a very large valley.

I could feel my mind expanding across the now open fields as I descended the gentle slope. A joy was invading my soul and I enjoyed the freedom this view offered.

The descending slope revealed a vast flat plain, expanding before me. Upon closer inspection the soil was black. This could only mean that it was a river flat. Yet I could not see a river, so vast was this plain. Agriculture abounded, lucerne, vegetables, cereals and livestock. A food bowl revealed itself before my eyes.

To my right the flat plain extended. The river must've been in that direction, out of sight. To my left a small hill rose, as if to be a sibling to the one I had just descended. As I glanced upon the slope of this hill, there stood two ornate early Victorian mansions. The view from these dwellings would have been magnificent. Given their age they were possibly the result of successful pioneers to this district.

The question then beckoned, what was this district like before the white man invaded? Certainly these two rather English looking buildings would have been very out of place to what the landscape was. They seemed to exhibit a mystery, unknown facts, that intrigued me.

A railway line now ran parallel to the highway, to my left. So close at times that its presence held command. The mansions were now lost from view by the embankment of the railway line, obscured by progress.

Still the onslaught of on-coming traffic continued. If anything increasing, where were they all coming from?

The embankment levelled out so as I could see the left side scenery. On the far side of this view portrayed a shape that could be indicative of only one activity. A water reservoir poked itself above the savannah in the shape of a wine glass. I had seen these before. They were standard issue to all military bases. So this area was protected by the armed forces. Maybe this was where all these cars were coming from? The answer was quickly answered as I passed an intersection with a sign pointing to an army base, but no excess of cars filing from this road leading to the right. The army base was not the reason for all these cars heading opposite me.

As suddenly as it appeared the railway line to my left headed to another direction, away from the highway. I noticed billboards, some professionally done, and some with, "thumb nail dipped in tar". They were all displaying seemingly important information about ways for the travellers to part with their money. This could only mean one thing, which was confirmed with a speed limit sign reading 80 km/hour. I was entering a town.

The paddocks gave way to businesses. Car sale yards, motels, service stations, all lined the thoroughfare as to herald that this was a town of significance. Another indication was that, although I had had a good run coming into the town, it had now stopped. Stopped it was for no visible reason, just stopped. The little traffic I had encountered travelling in my direction had now trapped me in. On the other side of the road the steady stream continued as like a river with a leaking reservoir as the head water.

Moving again, slowly, it soon became apparent why the slow

down. Two sets of lights now appeared and I wondered if I should be able to get through them both before the lights changed. No such luck, stopped again.

It was obvious that this highway was the greatest obstacle in this town. Any good travelling time made before this town was now lost by the congestion the highway presented. I wondered what the local people thought of this maze of metallic boxes invading their space on a regular basis.

I had been driving for long enough on this day, the sun was getting low and time for a break. I had no deadline to keep and this town seemed like a suitable resting place. I wanted to see what this town was like away from the highway.

The dual traffic lights loomed, still green, but I could see, once past them that the congestion continued. I had had enough. Capturing the first of the lights I indicated a left turn to hopefully lead me to see what this town was really like.

This new street was lined with houses. Nothing elaborate but certainly a different style to what I had been used to in Sydney. Each house displayed a different design and thus seemingly, personality. Their age varied and this seemed to give an indication to their character. They all had large spacious yards, as opposed to the multi congestion of Sydney dwellings I had come from. I envisaged this extra room to the abodes gave rise to happier inhabitants. It was a long street with stop signs on the cross streets, registering that this street was of importance.

In the distance I could see that the street was going to end in a "T" intersection. It loomed at an angle. Not knowing the local rules I thought it prudent to turn left as that angle was broader. Looking to my right it became obvious that his was the main street, with lots of shops, cars and people. Further there was a large shopping centre opposite. I turned left and spying a park on the right beyond the shopping centre, decided that was where I wanted to go. Indicator on I waited for a taxi to turn right in the direction I wanted to go. I followed this vehicle till it turned into the shopping centre. I wondered upon the people the driver had encountered on this day's driving. What the driver had learnt about this town.

The greenery of the park revealed itself as well as a little road that lead into the park proper. That is where I went and parked under a large deciduous tree enjoying the new growth spring had provided. I could feel the peace of this place invading my soul. I was becoming more relaxed again. The solace I had found had slowed time to the extent that it was no longer relevant.

The spell was being bought back to reality by an invading noise that continued to grow. Behind me was the railway line which had obviously traversed around the town, and it was from there that this noise emanated. It became over powering and as the object of the noise became visible it revealed itself to be three locomotives pulling many and many coal trucks.

The riddle of the many and many cars heading east had been answered. Along with the obvious agricultural presence in this district and the army base, it was the coal in this area that gave it, its prosperity. When I was entering the town it must have been knock off time at the coal mines, hence the traffic congestion. The workers were heading east from their pit as their day's work headed east towards the port.

The Girl with the Burgundy Hair

Soft notes in a complex key creating a change of colour, of scene. The notes break the tedium of the summer's sun, like a fresh breeze of different thoughts. They present a new reality opposing the humdrum of convention.

Aimlessly to begin, different tones that may combine to say something, something undefinable at the conclusion. The questions remain. It is pleasant to hear, simple and neat in its material, but leaves lingering lethargy of wonderment and mystery. Who was Debussy referring to in "The Girl with the Flaxen Hair?"

The rounds of the new job, the meetings of soon to be workmates, the employer with his encouraging face covering his need for taxi drivers. The underlying thought of "You're going to like it here, look at all these great mates", please believe me.

"This is our administrator."

Her room was not dissimilar to his that I had just come from. An office now but was possibly, at some time, a bedroom. Small, cluttered, with stuff scattered, not really designed as an office but has evolved to be one out of necessity.

As opposed to the similarity of his office this one had some semblance of order. His desk was awash with papers in chaotic disarrangement, but doubtless to him quite ordered. In her office one could see the shining desk top of plastic wood. Items were piled to give the impression each pile had its reason.

She would've obviously heard our voices from the room, his office, just across the small and narrow corridor. The doors of these rooms were always open. However when I was shown into her office, she looked up surprised by the sudden intrusion.

She was seated behind the computer, obviously transfixed upon her task. Our presence broke the spell. In her confusion she might've stood, but instead of advancing upon introduction, retreated her movable chair away from her computer desk, retreating from our advance. Perhaps she felt safer to put distance between herself and these two bodies now imposing upon her space.

Her thick almost curling but certainly naturally tightly woven hair was tied together by a band at the back of her head. Although her attire would be seen to have been out of place in a modern city office, in this small country business it was quite acceptable. It was very casual, her jeans were loose and her green jumper, perhaps a couple of sizes too big, covered her obviously thin body.

With a slightly bent back she stood almost apprehensively waiting for the progress in the interaction. Why this shyness? What was being hidden? Questions opened. Her smiles covered up walls that as yet could not be seen nor understood.

Forms to be filled, information to be conveyed, the boss exits and the formalities begin. Two strangers were now physically closer for reasons of convenience. The vibes were yet to be understood. A sense of uneasiness still invaded not by way of threat but simply a degree of shyness as ignorance about each other.

Keeping to the message and in a truly professional manner she asked her questions methodically as if it had been done before. Her aged would've been at least ten years more than mine, more evident by her diligence to her task. Although it assured me of her competence it also displayed a certain genuineness in her character. A positive attitude conveyed through gentleness and truth.

In answer to one of her questions I searched through my passport. Mistakenly I showed her the wrong page. She questioned me about the Russian visa on this particular page.

"Oh," she said with surprise. "You've been to Russia?"

"Yes, I spent six days on the Trans Siberian railway from China. Then I spent time in Moscow and St Petersburg."

"I've heard St Petersburg is very beautiful?"

"One of the most beautiful cities in the world. I really liked Russian architecture, the Hermitage, the canals, a stunner of a city."

"Wasn't it cold?"

"I was there in April but I did encounter a day of blizzard on the train. It must look so pretty in winter as the buildings are painted in such gay pastel colours. They would give brightness in the bleakness of winter. You wouldn't catch me there in winter though. I hate being cold. Have you travelled?"

She paused before answering. The expression on her face told of a great regret even before she spoke.

"No, but I've always thought that I would like to one day."

I continued a little rave about my travels. Her now willing eye contact and enthusiasm to my tale showed a certain willingness to let go, a very little bit, the tight walls which were confining her. The stranger now had definition to her and she found him interesting. I could see her imagination grow as my tale of my travels continued. Whether her fantasies were true to my words or a variation to what she would have imagined, I don't know. Certain my little rave had created in her a travelling experienced she had possibly never had. It seemed weird to me that I, the much younger, was much more worldly. It should've been the other way around. Why?

She told me of her little farm where she looked after her parents and her horse. The latter seemed to give her more joy. It was far removed from St Petersburg yet by the pride she showed in her home and her situation I somehow like to feel she had possibly found her place of St Petersburg. Yet I don't know. Questions still lingered.

It is a simple melody conjuring images of beauty and unexplained fantasies. Conveyed by seemingly complex but easy pentatonic scales, diatonic chords and plagal leading notes, it is pleasant to hear but leaves me wondering. Who is this girl with the burgundy hair?

Scott, part 2

After my tuition upon driving taxis I would come back to the park where I had arrived in this town. I saw it as a place of reflection, an open space to let my mind wander freely.

I had decided that this town was to be home for a time. Never one to be too fussy about my abodes, it was basically a place to sleep and eat. I had found a small flat in a less than fashionable street. It was a one bedroom affair with a room that doubled as a living space, kitchenette and a place to plonk things. The walls were painted some time ago when it was fashionable to have dull colours, browns, greys and a little faded yellow as highlights. As a rental the owners must have decided that an update of the interior was not economically viable. It did have a small space to call a garden even if the plants were in pots. The rent was cheap and it served the purpose. I only had myself to worry about and I never wanted for much.

I had discovered that on the western side of the park the river ran. It had been avoiding view as I entered the town but now visible by its influence, it formed an integral part of the landscape. I had notices that the roses in this town were particularly vigorous in their growth. They were growing on prime river flats.

There was not much flow in this river. The water flowed past lazily. However by the high banks the river had carved out it was obvious that this was not always the case. To my right were two bridges that transcended the water course. One, the further one, was much newer than the other and was constructed with cement. It conducted the highway traffic, the ones just passing through to another destination. Oblivious to the river they were crossing, those travellers kept their focus upon their destination. They were moving. The older bridge, which possibly was the route of the highway originally, showed its age. The iron pillars were rusted and the wooden roadway protested about still being used. Although not as much traffic used it, when they did the groans it produced gave testimony to its age. This bridge was obviously used only by the locals, possibly out of habit, where it formed a part of their lives cyclical patterns.

The large park land around me gave an imminence of tranquillity. Sporting fields predominated, which laid the foundations of enjoyed hours for the inhabitants of this small town. It was nice to be in the country side again.

Gone were the hectic days in Sydney, being a salesman in a tiling warehouse. Gone were the days of practising the persistence of the perpetual fake smile, the sales targets that always had to be reached. Gone were the lies that had to be said to satisfy the corporation. The fake conversations listened to that had to be endured. The snarling faces on the street too preoccupied with vanity to notice if it was light or night. Each had their own constructed wall to keep at bay the others that want to invade. Trapped inside their own cocoon, they will never experience the peace to be attained from the Sunyata. They were never to experience Nirvana.

My soul was trapped into conventionality and my spirit was waning. I was now in my early thirties. I needed to experience more of this life than being trapped into a negative routine. I needed to find my peace again. Connect with my soul. It wasn't going to happen in a city. The stillness of the country, the trees, the birds, the silence, creates a suitable environment for ones well being. I felt free. I felt happy. I was peaceful again. I began to enter that state of mind which I had trained for in the Himalayas. I was in search of perfection and to experience that exquisite peace that can only come from within.

It wasn't going to happen in this western world that I had been bought up in as a child. It was a stingy little apartment in an inner western suburb of Sydney. So old as to have lost count of the number of families it had housed. It was the bottom dwelling and as such often smelt and housed different types of mildew depending upon the weather conditions. The building obviously once housed a very wealthy family at the turn of the twentieth century. The staircase above us would've been an ornate feature in its day. In our time it showed the scares of uncaring tenants. Its glory days pasted when a developer turned it into several apartments.

I never knew my father. Although my mother never wanted to divulge much about the circumstances of my conception, I learned, in a roundabout way, that my conception was the result of casual meeting at a party. That was as much as I ever knew. I never knew his name. I don't know if he's in Australia. I   often fantasise that one day, in my travels I might stumble upon this father of mine. That's perhaps when a lot of questions would be answered. Perhaps then my life would gain some stability. I would have a model. I would know where I stood. In the mean time I kept searching for something I couldn't define.

My mother did the best that she could to bring up her only child. She would sometimes work a night shift when I would be asleep. At the time I thought it was normal but as experience has taught me, she must've had a difficult existence. She showed me the love that only a mother could give, on the surface. However I often thought that I was a burden in her life. She died of cancer when I was sixteen. Her sister wanted me to come and live with them. However that lingering thought that I

17

would only become another burden didn't appeal. I didn't like school and was old enough to leave. The big world outside with lots of questions to be answered seemed a much better alternative.

So my wandering life began. I was looking for answers to questions, in search of something that I didn't understand, trying to understand my place in this existence. The conventional idea of a steady job with a trapping debt was never my go. I had other motives. It was not to be found in a western culture. As a young man I found it ridiculed with directives upon the rules one's life should be conducted. All for the good of the mortgage, the employer, trapped in a capitalist system of forever wants. Peace will not come out of stress. I was in search of another system so I travelled. Seeking work with whatever I could find, each held its own set of experiences, till I had saved enough to move onto the next place.

My time in India had enlightened my soul. It had answered many questions. I had found some stability that would form a bed rock to my time in this space.

Perhaps this little rural town would be another experience to add to my already colourful tapestry of life. Perhaps I might be able to expel unto others the peace to be obtained from within one's soul. The only good we can do in our lives is to do good to others. Anything else is sheer vanity. Perhaps I might be able to answer some of my questions.

Shane

The officers in charge had deemed it appropriate that the recruits could be allowed out of the military camp, this week end.

I found myself, now as a trained taxi driver, having to do overtime on this Saturday night.

The recruits, many of them barely out of high school, had been stuck in this camp for months as a result of the COVID situation. In that time they had been isolated from their families, their friends, their natural environment, their comfort zone. Instead they had been subjected to mindless discipline and exhausting treks through the bush with full packs on. They had been surviving the elements of cold, fatigue and inner strength. Endless weapon drills and monotonous parade marching.

Their previous years were now history and this new stage of their existence was being filled with a new family of mates, enforced companionship which was vital to their survival. From everywhere in Australia they came. From different surrounding they came. From unique social circumstances they arrived at this camp. All were to be unified under the one banner. With glee and positivity they have surrendered themselves to this "career".

Their naivety was plain to see to us who are much older. Once they sent boys like this to Vietnam and other slaughter houses to fight other people's wars. After the conflict, they expected them to live normal lives.

A steady stream of calls to the camp had been presented in the earlier evening. Excited testosterone driven young men, filled with the fantasies that a small country town might unfold. They had been filling into the maxi taxi for hours en route to the closest dream delivering destinations.

By nine pm it was to be realised that the images of freedom, imagined over the previous weeks, were now being activated by a never diminishing schooner glass. Then another call out to the army camp logged. It was deemed to be later than usual with the night now in full progress. Out along the dark and lonely country drive that led to the isolated post, I treasured the contact that the night presented. The lights of the entrance became apparent and soon the solace of the darkened night would soon be severely altered by very large search lights. The security guard looked sternly as the maxi taxi approached, then was reassured that the vehicle followed the usual path.

A group of boys, excited voices, had assembled and were gratified to see their transport arrive. They approached with a knowing recognition that this was for them. They were in a hurry to catch up on missed time and opportunities.

"Good evening, sir," was the usual response in recognition of this human that was taking them to their freedom. They filed in with respect and although excited, paid courtesy, ordered into them, to the civilian.

Personally I didn't much care to be called "Sir". I didn't see myself as superior to these soldiers in making. However it had to be realised these boys were coming from a culture of superiority. They were at the bottom of the list, and they knew it. Thus their "sirs" had to be tolerated.

The energy in the confined maxi taxi had certainly changed from the solitude of the country road. The boys sorted out their seating arrangement without much reference. All seemed seated, yet there was a hesitation. I asked if we were ready to go.

"Another couple to come yet sir."

I waited, and they waited even more patiently than I. It was as though whoever was to arrive held some importance. Out of the darkness that hid the path to the barracks two figures emerged. Both walked with intent, purpose and with military precision as though they held the plans for the night's assault. They walked directly towards the bus and I started up the engine assured that these two were the delay.

The one in front walked much more boldly than his companion. His blond hair stood out almost charismatically under the weak lighting that displayed the control post.

Shane entered the taxi first as though he was the General in charge. His gaze centred squarely upon the taxi driver. I felt his piercing glare as if he was looking right into my inner sole. I was experiencing a "sus out" in the extreme. I felt a little intimidated if not invaded. But keeping to my role, as a defence, I concluded quickly that this was an alpha male to be respected as such.

He filled the seat closest to me, which was the central position in this bus, and turned his gaze towards the other bodies in the van. Their muffled chatter whilst they were waiting had turned to a personalised gab fest dictated to by Shane. Although being the same rank as the other recruits he certainly did command attention to his presence. They listened with intent as Shane issued his directives.

Into to the blackened night the maxi taxi began its journey along the darkened road towards the town that was to give these boys their moments of fantasy. Although the light in the taxi was rather dim, Shane's voice gave clarity to the situation. His dialogue ruled, although occasionally dispersed with comments from the other boys, his voice was their answer. So ruthless was his determination to be the leader of the pack it almost became aggressive. The alpha male was asserting his control with such intensity that I felt again threatened by this dominant fellow. I sure wanted to be on his side in any disturbance.

Now that they were off the camp, and safe from the constant scrutiny, the conversations became opinionated. Not, as expected, sour comments upon their toils over the last weeks but rather who was not standing up to the pressure. Obviously it was not "cool" to mention their inner struggles, given their new environment, but rather to comment negatively upon the ones who might be struggling with the ordeal. Social pressure was actively being applied to overcome weaknesses. As was now usual, Shane had the deciding opinion.

"He really needs to smarten himself up."

As the lights of the town encroached the darken path to illuminate the destination, chatter changed topic and different scenarios developed as fantasies. Each destination discussed, had its own dream and differing opinions filtered nervously around the interior. Shane listened as a good leader should but when the decision had to be made it was his suggestion that ruled without objection.

The pub chosen was one of the more popular ones in town. It had a reputation for being a bit rough but there were plenty of girls there. Its darkened interior could give camouflage to the realities of their work place. It offered the hope of a different existence to what they had been used to for so long.

As the bus stopped they quickly rose from their seats with military promptness. They paused to wait for Shane to lead them off the transport. There were groups of men there at the pub of differing social memberships, some with short hair, others with longer hair. They all peered at the taxi to see who would emerge. Universally they were delighted to see Shane's appearance. He had even transfixed the locals and not just his fellow recruits. With his arrival there seemed to be an optimism that the party was now really going to start.

The boys paid respects to me, the driver, but I was instantly forgotten in the excitement of the start of their night. I hoped they would enjoy this small town's nightlife. I hoped that they would never have to suffer the hideousness of battle, but if they did I wanted Shane to be on our side. He was a soldier and a natural leader of men.

Paul, part 1

There is a section of this country town, the north side of the highway, where the architecture was much older. No modern bricks but rather, in the most part, stone. The houses and the blocks that they were on were much bigger. The trees were well established and covered the roads. The yards always looked cared for and the gardens established. It was the elite section of the town.

It was also very adjacent to the hospital. It was said that a lot of the homes were built by rich doctors. When one had a call to this part of the town, manners were on display.

A call came from a Paul at one of the streets in this section. It was a quiet street, the end of which transformed into a cricket field. There was no through traffic.

I pulled up outside the address. The house was covered in weatherboard, prodigiously glossed in sparkling white paint. It had obviously been very well cared for given its older design. The garden, well established, had matured to express the full grandeur it was intended to display. Being mid spring the azaleas were in full bloom. They adorned the footpath leading to the front door. The spectacular colour, emphasised by the mid day sun, they created gave a welcoming to this charming old house. An open verandah bordered the building, adorned with a series of pot plants. By its prettiness and obvious care for detail it emitted a sense that a woman had expressed her desires. From where the taxi was parked, I could see the western side of the house. The end of the verandah, on this side, was walled to display what looked to be a study. The door was open onto the verandah and I peered into the room to see a man sitting quietly. He noticed the taxi's arrival and instantly arose as if he was anxious to begin his journey.

He appeared to lock the door from the study and proceeded, newspaper in hand, along the verandah. His walk was slightly hunched with small steps that by their slightness appeared to project him with haste as if they knew the routine. His eyes were fixed to the ground as if to aid in his navigational concentration towards his destination. He was not a tall man, in fact, his build was quite slight. He bore no extra weight as many men of his age do, in what appeared to be his sixties. He wore a sports jacket, maybe a little too big for his bodily size. It was a mixture of colours, mainly brown, faun and yellow. It resembled a garment which would have been quite stylish forty years ago, but now it only displayed a link to a more distinguished past. It did however give the appearance of the wearer that it was quite up market and gave him a certain element of class. His brown trousers hang off his waist with the help of the invaluable brown belt. His shirt was rather out of place being blue. It didn't quite fit the rest of his attire. No tie and open at the collar. It was as though this shirt was the only alternative, odd looking as it was.

He proceeded through the open gate with no intention of closing it. His mind was on other things. He had to veer a little to his left to approach the taxi. He didn't make a visual decision to do this. It was as though he knew where to go.

When he was in closest proximity to the taxi and he knew he had to be assimilated to a seat. His first impression was to go to the front seat. However he realised, after seeing my face peering through the glass, that this was, in fact, a driver he had not yet encountered.

He hesitated with indecision. The COVID restrictions were in force and it was deemed to be safest for the passengers to sit in the back. Obviously, since this was a driver that he had not met previously and in order to do the right thing, he made his decision. He opened the door to the back seat and looked up at his driver sheepishly.

His bright blue eyes shone brightly through the half closed eye lids. His face was wrinkled possibly beyond his years, but the beacons that were his eyes showed a yearning for life.

He looked at me with shyness which unveiled a certain insecurity. It did not make me feel uncomfortable. I could sense a joviality beyond the uncertainty. It led me to believe that this passenger could get a laugh out of me. He certainly had that "this is a character" appeal to him.

He climbed into his seat as though the new position was a completely different experience. I bid him good morning, as it was still just morning but he was too preoccupied with his frustration upon getting the seat belt to lock to reply.

When he was settled he looked up at me again quizzically and asked, "I never seen you before?"

I answered, "I'm Scott, I only just started a couple of weeks ago."

"I'm Paul."

"Where are we off to, Paul?"

His reply was quite a surprise to me. Given that he lived in a rather posh part of the town. Given that his attire resembled that of a private school graduate, he asked to be taken to one of the more daggier pubs. However, to be noted, this particular pub was the one that was the closest to his home.

"You're garden is looking fantastic," I stated as a conversation starter. "It must keep you busy, looking after it all."

"I don't do anything to it. That's the wife's domain."

"It must keep her busy then?"

"No, she's off in London at the moment. She's organised some bloke who comes around on Mondays and potters about around the place. I don't have anything to do with him. It's nothing to do with me."

"What's she doing in London?"

"She an executive for some big company, and had to go to a meeting there, or something."

"Didn't you want to go as well?"

"No, London's a cold miserable place. I'm staying here where the sun does shine."

He settled into his back seat, mask secured and I set the vehicle in motion for its purpose.

I could feel him sussing me out but words could not come to his aid. I felt he wanted to break the ice with this new driver who seemed friendly enough but his shyness prevented him.

As the football finals were now in progress and to break the ice, I asked him which team he went for. It was an open question as I did not know which brand of football he followed.

"Couldn't give a stuff," was his reply. "My team aren't there so who cares?"

"Which team do you go for?"

"Carlton."

I now knew he preferred Australian Rules football.

After a bit of a silence he asked, "Who do you go for?"

The only thing I knew about Aussie rules was that the fans were very parochial. The wrong reply would've been fatal. I chanced one name that I knew of.

"St Kilda."

"Thank goodness for that I was worried it would've been Collingwood. I hate Collingwood."

"So do I."

"Youse are all right, you haven't won a premiership in decades."

The conversation lulled at the set of lights which always seemed to be red when ever this intersection was reached.

To ease the impatience I asked, "What's on at the pub?"

"Lunch."

The reply suggested that this conversation starter wasn't going to be expanded.

Destination reached and money exchanged, I asked, "What's for lunch?"

"Three schooners of VB."

With that his body moved inconspicuously into the hotel.

Ryan

It was common knowledge, amongst the taxi drivers that I worked with, that certain addresses were dreaded. One such address was in the heights. With this address however there were two respondents, one good, one bad. It was a guess which respondent one was going to cop.

The house was inhabited by Alice, a woman in her thirties with young children. Also living at this address was Alice's brother, Ryan. Ryan was the bad one.

Ryan would have been in his late twenties. A very small man, by his very size a vocational adviser would have instantly sectioned him off as a jockey. Whether he had any ability with horses would not have mattered, he had the physical attributes.

But given that a prerequisite to being a jockey was kindness to all, especially horses, this was never going to happen. He was a very sour, self abscessed little man with not much going for him as a result.

He was a talking point amongst the other drivers. It was an amusing game to compare which driver he had been rudest to. I had heard these reports before I had actually to encounter him. But upon hearing these reports I wondered if he could be that bad. I had learnt during my studies in India that there is goodness in every one. Therefore there must've been a key to Ryan. Given my insistence in my own tolerance I was in anticipation upon our meeting. Perhaps I could help him.

It was a bright and sunny mid Saturday morning. The

shoppers were now busy. The junior sporting teams were assembling. The day was now active. A call came from an address in the heights. It was not familiar to me. I arrived at this smart looking house, similar to the other newer smart houses in the area. They had tidy, cut lawns, nothing laying about the place, cultivated gardens, newer houses, very normal to this part of the town. It had the stamp of a financially viable middle class area.

I slowed to a stop and noticed a little man waiting on the front porch. He saw me and advanced with purpose towards the taxi. He carried a device with him that was emitting noise. The determined look on his face did not show any emotion or social grace. In fact, he looked quite angry. His eyes were set on the back door and opened it with force. Positioning himself with purpose he did not hesitate to express his concern.

"How come it took you so long to get here? I booked this taxi over fifteen minutes ago."

It then occurred to me, from the description already given, that this was, in fact, Ryan. My ideologies were about to be tested.

He didn't seem to require an answer to his question but rather it was his way of expressing his frustrations. I also decided it needed no reply.

The noise of his device now became audible as the volume was up rather high. He seemed more interested in the voices via the airways than his immediate situation.

I set the car in motion and asked.

"Where are we off to?"

"The hospital," was his very curt reply, as though I should've known. He obviously hadn't taken into account that this taxi driver's face was a different one.

No conversation just listening to the radio, very loud. However, I was impressed with the subject matter of the interview. It was not your normal "fairy floss" commercial radio stuff of little significance, but rather an intellectual argument upon politics. It was not what I was expecting from the reports I had of Ryan. One of the voices made a very interesting argument. I chanced a comment.

"He might have a point there."

"What the fuck would you know? And shut up I can't listen while you're talking."

I spent the rest of the journey under imposed silence. We arrived at the hospital and a card was thrust in my direction. I fulfilled the necessary financial details and he left in silence.

"So that was Ryan," I thought as he walked up the path. Obviously he had a lot of in built anger and frustration. The effect was his bad manners, perhaps. It was the cause that I pondered upon. Treat the cause and there will be no effect.

A mid week call to the hospital around lunch time. Never knowing who it might be from the hospital, I arrived seeking out the client. It didn't take long to see the snaring face and distinctive little figure of Ryan progressing to the taxi.

I waited in anxious expectation but was determined to play "water off a duck's back" to any rudeness, to adhere to my pledge of tolerance. He clambered into the back seat.

"Home?" I asked politely.

His reply was not reciprocated with the same courtesy. Yes it was "home" but via a certain fast food outlet. I dreaded going to these places, the smell doing the drive through bit, the waiting and then the smell of the food in the car, was never a pleasant experience.

Almost as to be expected, there was a considerable line up

being the time of day that it was. The meter kept ticking though, only the smell and the impatience to tolerate.

I was curious to find out the reason for his frequent visits to the hospital? I chanced and dared a question to break the silence as we waited.

"How did you go at the hospital?"

"The usual."

I didn't learnt much and by the tone of the reply I wasn't ever going to. The section where one orders the food was drawing closer. I certainly didn't want anything but I wondered, since, Ryan was in the back seat, how the communication of wants was going to be carried out. Was I to be the portal of communication? Yes, I was. The voice on the intercom emitted its usual blurb and before I could answer I needed instruction from the back seat, not knowing what sort of rudeness this was going to inspire. With a reply needed, urgency usurped diplomacy.

"What do you want, Ryan?"

"The usual."

"What's that?" I asked without anger.

His list started and I related it to the voice on the intercom. It went on for quite some time and I wondered if the voice was collating all of this correctly.

When it was clear that the end of the wants were finished, as indicated by a cessation of noise from the back seat, I heard the voice on the intercom.

"Yes, proceed to the next window."

Realising the extent of the order, I anticipated a longer wait with the smell of the place becoming overwhelming.

Eventually, at the next window, the order was ready. Not without a considerable line up of cars behind us, waiting. The articles were handed to me one by one. Due to the extensiveness of the order the hand movements became automatic in repetition. There were hamburgers times a few, each with a different specification, packets of chips, drinks times two, sweet things, more chips and nuggets. How could such a slight human consume such a load?

Ryan inspected each package as it was delivered. I hoped there was nothing wrong. Dreading his temper if it wasn't right. It wasn't. His temper and loud aggressive voice imposed itself with great force.

"I asked for no gherkins on this burger. Can't these people ever get it right?"

It was obvious that the young person delivering the goods could hear all that Ryan was exclaiming. We were both feeling a little embarrassed and generally awkward. Ryan thrust the package back to me.

"Tell them I want another one, with no gherkins on it this time. Christ can't these people get it right."

I turned to the young, now a scared employee, and in as soothing and calm a voice as I could muster.

"Would you mind getting another one please, with no gherkin on it?"

The eyes of the young attendant and mine met and with an understanding of the situation. A communication was had. Ryan and I waited, again for the right product.

Breaking the silence was a tirade from the backseat.

"What is wrong with these young people? Why can't they transfer the information correctly? Are they that stupid? Can't they make a note of the order and then check it out to see that everything is correct? It's not as if they are discovering the workings of dark matter. Just listen and get it right."

That was only the beginning of the consistent rant from the back seat. It continued on and on, repeats after repeats, sometimes increasing in anger to a crescendo, testing my patience, only to be broken by the eventual appearance of the revised product. I passed it to the back seat for inspection and after a considerable pause.

"They got it right at last for a change."

With that I chanced a glance at the young attendant, indicating, "Well done." To which the young person chanced a slight smile.

Conscious of the other cars, who had been waiting patiently, I moved off as quickly as I could. Soon to be hit with the smell of the food. Ryan had not hesitated in devouring the food he had ordered. It was company policy that food was not to be eaten in the taxis. From the smell of this food it was a good policy which we all adhered to. The revolting smell compelled me to make a comment, despite the possible negative circumstances.

"Ryan, you are not allowed to eat in the taxi."

"You dumb bastard. I have too. Don't you understand?"

By the force of his delivery and his arrogance upon regulations, I realised that I would have to tolerate his woofing into his hamburger with no gherkins, then the chips and the drink with the compulsory and loud slurping at the end of the container. My personal appetite had been nullified by the animalistic consumption from the back seat.

I was grateful for the teaching from my gurus in India in that I could be tolerant and calm in such a situation which might cause others to be aggressive. To meet a negative with another negative till all disintegrates. It is a wise and just person that can turn a negative into a positive.

Besides there was a cause to this effect being constantly emitted from the back seat and I wanted to help this soul. Walls needed to be broken.

"Do you like living in this town?"

"It just is."

Although, in character the answer was nasty, it wasn't what I was expecting. I paused for a bit, not certain which way to steer the conversation. His mouth was still being forcefully invaded by substances some call food.

"It's a pleasant town. So what's on for the rest of the day?"

The reply didn't come instantaneously and I was hoping I might've hit a soft spot in his portrayed anger. I was wrong.

"You want me to talk. Just how stupid are you? Can't you see that I'm eating? How can I talk with a mouthful?"

The eating continued for the rest of the journey. The card was thrust into my immediate presence. Transactions completed without a word spoken.

As he left I chanced "I hope you enjoy the rest of the day."

I heard again, "It just is."

Another time I was called to the address. It was a Saturday morning and I was in a maxi taxi. Never knowing who was going to be the client I drove sceptically.

It was just as well that I was in the maxi taxi, the whole household was waiting. Alice, all her children and Ryan were forwarding down the driveway.

Alice was a happy person. She emitted a joy to be alive and always a pleasant conversation. Very different to her brother, I wondered upon the dynamics of this combination.

Alice was her bubbly self as they approached the van. She fossicked about caring for her children and greeted me with courtesy. Ryan was very silent and seemed to accept the second fiddle role. However his vibe indicated an elephant in the room. All were settled and the journey to the supermarkets was in progress. Ryan appeared to be rather sulky in his manner. There was an impression that something was going to erupt.

One of the children became restless and was imposing herself upon Ryan's space. Ryan, self orientated and totally self obsessed as usual, called objection to this interference.

"Get away from me."

The child was frightened by the sudden outburst. Alice did not hesitate in her reply.

"Shut up Ryan. She's not doing you any harm."

She delivered her command with surprising and in a way, "out of character" venom. It took me by surprise. It did however have an immediate effect upon Ryan. He obeyed without hesitation.

I pondered this interaction. Was this the way to treat Ryan? With such force as to defeat him at his own game? Was it necessary to have absolute domination over the threat? It did seem to work though, but was it compassionate? Was it helping Ryan?

Some weeks later sitting in the maxi taxi assigned to me on this day, a call came from that address in the heights. Who was it going to be this time? If it was Ryan, what strategy would I have to employ?

I arrived at the address and watched who would alight from the door, psyching myself up with alternative methods for social interaction depending upon who would emerge.

Alice and the children emerged seemingly well rehearsed upon the day's actions. The group didn't include Ryan. As usual she greeted me kindly and the children were respectful. I didn't feel any anxiety of who was the outcome of personnel to be encountered this time.

All settled the journey was in place. My curiosity

overwhelmed me given that I had been prepared for the Ryan onslaught and I wondered upon Ryan's well being.

"How's Ryan?" I asked.

There was a slight hesitation in Alice's reply, as though I had mentioned a subject that was now of seemingly little significance.

"Ryan died a few weeks ago." She replied as though it was a matter of fact and of no emotional value. Her attitude surprised me. I was rather shocked by this news. She must've felt this in me and decided upon an elaborate.

"Ryan was always on borrowed time. It was always going to happen and he knew it. He fell of a horse when he was young. It damaged his kidneys. That's why he had to go to the hospital so often. He had to go onto the dialysis machine regularly. Then, that was not even enough to save him."

Many weeks passed. I was waiting in the cue at the taxi rank. I, being the third in the cue, had a bit of spare time. It was customary for the drivers in the cue to sometimes assemble outside the first driver's door for a chat. They were pleasant chats and good to associate with the ones doing the same as me.

After realising Ryan's demise and considering his reputation before his death I chanced a reference to him.

"At least we don't have to put up with his eating that disgusting food in the taxis anymore," was a reply.

"Did you have to put up with that as well?"

"We let him do that because he was a special case. You see he needed that food after the hospital to get his sugar levels up again."

"No more of that sort of carry on any more." Was another reply and the subject was dropped as Ryan filed into unwanted history.

Mrs Bowman Street

It was a Saturday afternoon in late November. Summer was making its presence felt. The air conditioner in the sedan taxi had been running all afternoon. There was only a couple of hours to go. The end of the shift was insight.

Again I angled the taxi into the shopping centre towards the taxi stand. Dodging other cars trying to find a parking space amidst the chaos this badly designed parking area had to offer. With the taxi stand in sight I had to wait, along with others behind me, for a large four wheeled tank to fit into a limited in size, space. At the third attempt from the four wheeled shiny metallic box that moves our passage was clear. Whilst waiting, I could see a familiar figure waiting on the taxi stand seats.

I steered the taxi into our inlet of sanctuary apart from the chaos of cars. The figure recognised the vehicle returning and began to assemble the objects attained from her shopping.

It was not surprising to see this particular figure. She was instantly recognisable. This was the usual time of the Saturday afternoon that she required her lift home.

Placing the car into park, opening the boot, I alighted from the car to help her with her groceries. She couldn't have noticed my approach as she was surprised to see another set of hands appear to assist her.

Her elderly body erected itself from its stooped position with hesitation that only an aged body does. Her wrinkled face looked at me blankly until a faint nod of the head showed recognition. No words were spoken and her weary face held no expression. Yet she did hold herself with a certain dignity though.

I could gather most of the plastic bags leaving her with a couple of lighter ones and one large box.

"You'll have to come back for that box, it is too heavy for me."

I placed what I had into the boot, in a hurry as to be able to open the back door for her. Her stooped body was about to open the door when my hand had reached across for the task.

Leaving her to place her body into the capsule of the taxi, I fetched the large box. It was obviously an electronic component of some sort. It was hard to place this lady with a modern devise, but there it was.

Ready to face the parking mess of indecisive drivers outside the taxi bay, masks correctly fitted I was about to place the vehicle into drive. Always check if the passenger is ready. I should've realised this as this lady always had trouble with the seat belt. It wasn't as though she was overweight. In fact the opposite was more accurate. I often wondered if she feed herself correctly, she was so thin.

I turned to see how she was progressing. It was her loosely clad dress that seemed to be the hindrance. At the point where I considered alighting to her assistance, she solved the riddle of the dress and the sseat-belt-belt. All comfortable, her mask adjusted, the taxi went into drive.

There was a certain feeling of relaxation emulating from the back seat. She was on her way home. The trials of facing the public with their consistent bad manners and lack of respect for the elderly, had taken its toll. The sanctuary of her little flat in a back street now proved to be the escape she was seeking.

She sat silently, alone in her thoughts, and never a smile to be expressed.

To avoid the role play of the taxi man, I would try a little conversation. Certainly there were no philosophical discussions. Rather a discussion upon the heat of this day, to break the silence. There was never much of a reply, as though she wanted me to stay as just the taxi man.

This time, however, I used my initiative to find a different topic which may give rise to a different response. I recalled the box that I had handled. Curious upon its utilisation and not knowing much about this lady, I assumed that it might have been a present. Christmas was looming.

"Have you started doing your Christmas shopping then?" I asked as an ice breaker.

A silence commenced, almost as though she had not heard the question or rather didn't want to converse. I felt a tinge of embarrassment but should've realised that she was contemplating her reply.

"Yes," she replied after a considerable pause. This led to another pause as I waited for elaboration.

"My grandson is into all this electronic games and stuff. I don't know much about it but the man in the shop said this is what they are all buying this year. I hope he likes it."

I was surprised at this sudden relaxation of the walls. I was not going to waste such a golden opportunity to find out more about this lady who had always kept herself to herself.

Although it was usually not the done thing to converse and relate to the taxi man, the joy of her purchase compelled her to express herself further.

"I just wouldn't know much about what they are into these days. I haven't seen them for so long. It's this COVID situation you know, we haven't been allowed to see each other for such a long time."

"Apparently they are going to relax the conditions coming into Christmas, where do your grand children live?"

"East of here towards the coast. It's about a three hour drive to get here."

"Will you be seeing them for Christmas?"

She paused before replying, as though she was trying to decipher reality from fantasies.

"I hope so."

The distance from the shopping centre to her street wasn't very far. The conversation had lasted the distance before I turned into her street. A dead end street lined with magnificent Jacarandas in full bloom, as if their bright purple blooms heralded the hope of Christmas.

Her small flat was on the left and I had remembered that there was a bit of a bump as one turned into her driveway. Cautiously I navigated the bump gently so as to make it as smooth as possible for her. The vehicle stopped appropriately. She stirred as the journey was now over. I alighted and opened the car door for her and helped her gain her feet.

I could tell that she wondered if I would help her with the groceries. To me it was a routine with this lady. She saw me fossicking around in the boot and she felt relieved. The route to her flat followed a cement path that winded itself towards the door. I knew a shorter way by steeping across the row of Azaleas to be in front of her slow progress. One load placed beside her door, I transgressed the Azaleas to get the second load.

By the time I had bought the second load up she had made it to the door. The usual practice was to leave her groceries at the door whereby she could sort them all out. But given that the box was a bit heavy I offered to bring it inside for her.

This was unusual. She pondered for a moment. A strange

man coming into her abode may have been her reasoning. Perhaps practically overcame convention.

"If you wouldn't mind."

She entered her flat and reached to keep the door open for me, loaded with the box.

I entered and as I did she stepped to one side. She pondered for a moment contemplating where to direct me.

It was a one bedroom flat. The door to the bedroom on the left was shut. The small but functional kitchen was immediately on my right as I entered this large room, which was the living area.

Veering to my left to avoid the kitchen area I entered a much more spacious area. At the end of the room the glass door opened up to a garden space outside. More Azaleas spreading the joy of Pascal colours shadowed and possibly out shone by an overhanging Jacaranda branch.

The room was adorned with furniture which would've been in vogue fifty years ago. They delivered an old worldly charm of curved wood and lacquer as opposed to the modern style of metallic straight objects.

High on the wall above one of these beautiful pieces of furniture was the picture of a young married couple, obviously this lady in her youth. It held pride of place. The couple looked so happy together as opposed to the expressionless face of this flat's current occupier. Underneath that photo, on a ledge that had been constructed for this task, were a series of photos of this lady cradling obviously her child. Next to each of these infant photos was a photo of that infant on their wedding day, many years later. The photos followed a time line that ranged from left to right, with the oldest child on the left. There were three such infant photos with the accompanying wedding photo. It was interesting to note the change of fashions from each era.

Underneath these series of photos, adorning the top of the sideboard, were a series of photos of the children each couple had produced. As to be expected the children corresponded to the parents above. Some couples had more than others. Each of this set of photos at all the different levels displayed such joy as to cast a wonderful positive energy into the room. They were certainly the centrepiece of the abode.

I could feel her pondering as I awaited further instruction.

"Just put it behind my chair, please."

A rather modern armchair placed facing the television in the corner with enough of a gap to the wall for the box to fit until, doubtlessly, it got covered with Christmas paper.

"Is there anything else I can do for you?"

"No thank you," was her immediate reply as though I was now an interference.

"I hope the COVID restrictions lift before Christmas and you'll be able to see your family again." I said leaving the flat.

"On well if they don't it will be much the same as last year then." She replied with a certain resignation to an existential outcome.

I left her to her solitude.

Iris

Before coal mining became the major industry and employer in the town, it was basically a rural community. The rich alluvial soils made it a haven for food production. The descendants of the pioneers had reaped the rewards of their predecessor's hard toil. Those that were now retired lived on the northern side of the highway. Their wealth was apparent. Their elitism was also obvious. Not wanting to let go of their traditional values and customs, they continued to hold themselves aloft from the usual people who lived on the other side of the highway. The proof of their apartheid was their high moral standing in the past and now present community. They knew the "right thing to do" opposed to those who lived on the other side of the highway.

They now had difficulty in accepting the change of their social structure with the influx of coal miners. To this emerging middle class injecting themselves into their sacred patch. They were not only destroying their land but also disturbing their elitist social structure. They bore the changes with a stiff upper lip and tolerance.

The north side of the town, the area near the hospital, was where the landed gentry had settled. Filled with squattocracy who were now retired from their rural properties, or where successful business people resided. It was a desired location.

In the bygone era, in which they still seemed fixed into, the south side of the highway would've been where the workers lived. It was a suitable distance apart to keep the social structure and order. These abodes were not so glamorous, in fact, the further south the less appealing the residences. In the era where social and housing development estates were established, there were located well to the south of the town.

One of these streets, lined with fibro housing development cottages was called Tuckan Avenue. The rentals on this area were the cheapest in town and thus attracted those looking for cheaper abodes. Unemployed, drug dealers, criminals and desperates inhabited this district. There were also those that lived a quite normal life restricted to this street by financial circumstances. But they were the quiet ones who lived in suspicion of everyone else in the street. Their suspicion was well foundered. During my induction as a taxi driver my instructors gave me fair warning of this thoroughfare. From my now experience of this street, their warning was well heeded.

In direct contrast to the well kept houses on the north side of the highway, these houses along Tuckan Avenue appeared to be in a constant state of chaos. Cynically I would remark to myself,

"A bit like India with no hope of enlightenment."

Disused junk would pile up on the side of the road waiting for brave council workers to pick it all up. It would stay there for months without a caring thought. Opened bonneted cars would stand idle for weeks waiting for an inspiration upon its repair. Unused toys, rubbish and objects of obscurity littered most lawns. There was no pride exhibited in these houses. They were walls to hide a depressed existence.

A call came on a Friday afternoon from the shopping centre to an address that I had become familiar with on Tuckan Avenue. The familiar figure of Iris was waiting for the taxi. She arose from the bench when she saw me arriving and started to arrange her many plastic bags of groceries. It was to be expected, it was a usual occurrence at this time on a Friday afternoon. I opened the boot and helped her with the bags. I was met with a simple but appreciative smile.

She was elderly. Difficult to exactly ascertain her age as her life's experiences had made their marks. She looked older than she possibly was. By the way she clasped her plastic bags it was obvious that she was frail. Her hunched back and the difficulty in walking under the load were the signs. I hurried to make her toil less arduous. She exhumed a kindness in her nature as though she naturally expressed the love she held inside of her.

By the time all of the bags had been loaded into the boot she was ready for a break. The back seat of the taxi relieved her toil.

"I've got the grand children coming over on the week end so I thought I'd best get extra stuff for them," she said wondering if I wondered over the excess bags this week.

I needed no directions to her address. A small fibro cottage with minimal garden but was painted a faded green to compensate. Its bareness made it distinguishable. Its humility did however seem to emit a type of contentment.

The house directly opposite, however, didn't exhume the same good vibes. It was shadowed by large trees which seemed to hide secrets. The paint, faded, was a mixture of blues, mostly dark. There was never a smile on the faces that I saw hanging around the place. Rather they were aggressive and paranoid faces which were presented to the street.

Upon first meeting her and realising her close proximity to the sleazy house I worried about her. It then became a regular topic.

"Did the electronic surveillance stuff work?"

"Well it worked but not for very long. Such nice chaps they were that come and did it. They showed me how it was working and all that before they left. I slept really well that night. Best I've slept for years. Then, when I woke up and checked it all out, it wasn't working. I went outside and noticed all the wires had been cut. I seen them, over the road, looking at the chaps when they were putting it all in. They knew what I was doing. I didn't hear anything because I slept so well. I hear them sometimes at night. They come through my backyard going to some place in the other street. I tried to fix up the back fence but that didn't last. I'm frightened to let the grand children play in the back yard cause you never know what might be there, that they've left. I'm still getting stuff that goes missing. I don't leave anything out doors now and at night I'm worried that one of them might come into the house. I keep it all locked and that, but you just never know."

"Could you call the police about them?"

"Oh no I wouldn't do that. None of us in this street would. We're all too scared of what they might do to us if any of us complained about them. We just try to ignore them, but they are always watching what's going on. Even when they are indoors, you think they are spying on us all. It's horrible."

"Do you ever think of moving?"

"Sometimes, but I don't want to. Me and my late husband bought up our family in this house, before they moved in. It's the only place I know as home."

We pulled into her driveway and I helped her with the groceries up to her door. She was very appreciative of my help and my ear.

"I hope you enjoy your grand children's visit,"I said in parting, trying to end the exchange optimistically. Inside, though, I felt worried for her.

Doug

I had learned that it was a good policy to train oneself to be rather a chameleon. Coming into contact with so many different types of people it was important to be on the same page as they are. It aids in making the interaction more intriguing as one learns much more by having the passengers know you can relate to them.

This newly acquired skill suited my situation and purpose. After my time in India learning under different and wonderful gurus, it was time for me to use my inner sanctum of tranquillity and experience life's many and varied stories. There's a lot to learn from these passengers. A lot of understanding of the human condition. Perchance, I might be able to spread a vibe of good will and inner peace, if they wish to find my page.

Or is it that only in my little abode, surrounded by walls, when I am by myself that I can truly be with myself.

Mid afternoon, a call came from an address in Tuckan Avenue. Apprehensive as to which assortment of a character I was going to encounter I ventured along the now very familiar path.

The house, corresponding to the number, showed the uniformity, with allowances for person taste and practicalities, of untidiness and lack of care. It was to be expected on this thoroughfare.

Hints about the occupants could often be detected by the stuff on the front lawns. For example toys indicated a family, etc. In search of a clue I noticed a considerable amount of rubbish laying about the premises, including beer cartons, cans and bottles. This gave a fair indication upon the residents.

A young man emerged from the front door, talking to someone inside with a very blokey voice. By the first impression, my hunch about the inhabitants was correct. It was a group of young men who were sharing this house. Thus they carried the carefree nature about them, this being the fun time of their early adulthood.

He walked down the path with an air of confidence and high self esteem. He was donned in shorts that had stains on it indicating a few days of wear. His tee shirt hung loosely from his shoulders as though it was used to this rather casual format.

As he approached he glanced at the taxi driver and decided the front seat was the go. The door opened with force and the taxi suddenly shook with the arrival of his body onto the seat, such was his eagerness. Soon after, it shuttered again with the closing of the door.

As he reached across to fix his seat belt he smiled at me. A welcoming smile which suggested he had a likeable personality. He made me feel at ease.

"Where are we off to mate?" I asked.

"Around to me mates place in Brigagee street. I don't know the number but I'll know the place when I see it."

I knew this street, it was not that far from where we were, but there were two ends to it and not knowing the number I had to guess from which end I was going to attack this street from. I chose the Main street entrance to the street and, when it was obvious which way I was going, there was no complaint.

It was a Friday, early afternoon. Most people would be at

work, excepting those on rostered systems, like those in the mines. He looked like he could fit into this category.

"Not working today?" I asked.

"No. Haven't got a job. On the dole at the moment."

"Looking for work?"

"Haven't got a licence to drive at the moment."

"How come?"

"Bastards took it away from me."

"How come?"

"DUI, driving without a licence, riding an unregistered bike, possession, drunk and disorderly."

"Bad night eh?"

"Real bad night. Lost me job. Had to move out of the place where I was staying..."

"Where are you staying now?"

"Sometimes with me brother but his girlfriend doesn't really want me there. She's nice enough but I can tell. Other than that, I've got a lot of mates that I go and couch surf at."

As we were passing the railway station where differing roads meet at differing angles, a bike approached dramatically from the road entering on my left. It took me by surprise and found that I had to brake suddenly so as not to collide. The rider took no notice of me and continued on.

"Ducati nine hundred" Doug voice sounded with envy and longing.

"I used to own one of those. I had to sell it. Bloody beautiful machine it was. Gets the chicks in, I tell you that. I used to love it when I had them as a pillion passenger. You'd look like you've taken the corner too fast and they'd panic and hold onto you even tighter. I loved that feeling, their thighs rubbing up against your bum. Really horny it was..."

The incident with the Ducati had obviously stimulated my passenger, Doug's, imagination or rather the memory of his fantasies. His preamble became increasingly sexist, to the point where I began to find it offensive.

I restrained my anger in the wisdom of tolerance and rather, listened to another person's reality in an effort to understand his world.

"I had a really hot one on me the night they pulled me over. She was all over me, really loved me bike, I was in for a really good night. The bastards were waiting for me near where I was staying. Some bugger must've dobbed me in when I did that wheelie down the main street. After that, never saw her again. No bike, no chicks, I suppose."

By this stage we had entered the destined street.

"Which house is it, mate?" I enquired.

He had been lost in his rave and suddenly had to assimilate where he was. It didn't take him long.

"Just up here, past this next intersection. You'll know it, it the one with all the rubbish outside it."

He was right and we pulled up outside a house that didn't look much different to the one I had picked him up from.

"This is the one."

He could see the fare and paid cash, always appreciated.

"Staying here the night?"

"No. Me mate that lives here needs a car. His missus is up the duff, due any day, and he hasn't got a car. So I'm giving him three grand to go and buy one."

"Generous of you."

"He needs it at the moment more than I. Its money from the

sale of me bike. I can't buy another one at the moment can I? So there. Besides, he's me mate."

"At least you'll have somewhere to stay tonight?"

"Could, I suppose. Met this chick at a mate's place yesterday. She gave me her address. Thought I might try me luck there."

Sarah

My journey through other people's experiences led me to wonder just how much control do they have over their lives? A life full of stimuli, their response follows. They have no power over the stimuli and thus no power over the response as a result of the stimuli. But these responses will indomitably alter their original plans. Moral, why plan?

A call came on a week day afternoon from a familiar address in Tuckan Avenue. It was never certain just how many would be picked up from this address. Luckily, on this day, I was in the maxi taxi so numbers would not be a question.

I had made it a habit to park in the driveway of this address. Sometimes it would be the grandmother who was not very flexible in her movements, or sometimes it would be Sarah with any number of her children.

Although this house was on the dreaded avenue and although this house showed the signs of neglect as if to obey the uniformity of the address' position in the town, it always, to me, gave a vibe of homeliness. It was the home of Sarah, her three little children and their grandmother and as such the homeliness atmosphere around the house prevailed.

It still didn't prevent the gauze door at the front from clanging in the wind, due to the fact that it was ill fitted. The roses along the front fence showing little interest in flowering due to the fact they never get pruned and the couch grass sucking out all the nutrients before them.

The gauze door opened without the wind's assistance. I recognised Sarah as she exited the house, backwards, a certain indication that there were more bodies to follow. Her scolding voice was another indication.

Soon after, the bodies of three little girls emerged from the house. Given prior knowledge I knew the oldest was six the other two were two years apart. The two year old, still struggling to understand walking, was assisted by the four year old. The six year old, Bec, walked without a smile and with rather a gloomy disposition.

Sarah walked with purpose as though there was a certain urgency, exemplified by her "hurry up" to the children. She glanced at me as she filed past the passenger's door and, after a slight recognition, opened the door of the van. Bec was waiting and filed in without instruction but with the gloomy face. It was obvious she didn't want to be a part of this exposition.

The two other children had arrived and Sarah helped them into the van. The tedious task of strapping them all in began. Due to the many rehearsals of this procedure in the past, it was performed quickly and efficiently by Sarah.

Bec, thinking she would be smart, tried to do it herself but was having difficulty. As Sarah was adjusting her apparatus, Bec in her disappointment of failing, sat gloomily as though she was brooding upon a new request.

"Mummy, are we going to get some of those lollies again like last time?"

"No."

"Oh. You said you would." Bec said as she tried hard to express ultimate disappointment.

"I can't afford them this week. I've only got ninety dollars to spend and that's got to get us through the whole week and pay for the taxi."

Sarah found her seat as Bec sank deeper into hers, with an extra gloomy face, and lips that pointed very much downwards. She was not happy and the determination on her face suggested that silence was the mode in which to express this.

All set, I reversed out of the drive way. I could feel the anxiety in Sarah's mood. She was never at ease but this time seemed to be acutely worse.

She was a very attractive young lady, no older than twenty five. Her long blonde hair, although currently looking rather untidy, could be made to look very appealing. A short lass and rather thin, I sometimes wondered if her thinness was a result of her poverty or just genetics. Perhaps it was a bit of both, in conclusion, after meeting her mother, "Nanny" to the children, for the first time.

By her manner of speaking she could come over as being a bit rough. I had learned that this was not necessary true. She possessed a certain refinement, good manners, to suggest she could do and say the right things at the right time. She was quite intelligent and I believed her when on a previous occasion she boasted about being one of the brightest in her form at high school. At one stage, given her abilities and looks, anything may have been possible for her. It would seem that her circumstances had led her to her street wisdom and current vocabulary. She once stated to me that she would've liked to have been a model. She would not have looked out of place in such a role. But at this moment her current circumstances had replaced her dreams.

The van, pointed in the right direction, meter on, passengers settled, the journey started.

"Things a bit tight at the moment?" I asked sympathetically.

A slight pause began where I believe she was trying to associate with this new verbal interchange that had interrupted her existential thoughts.

"Yeah a bit. We've got bills piled up, rent's overdue and princess here wants a bag of lollies."

"Can't her father help."

"You're kidding me. Him!" she said with anger.

"Haven't seen him in years. Bec wouldn't even know what he looked like. Bastard, he's still in town, I know that, but couldn't give a stuff about his kid."

"Is he the father of the other..."

"Only Bec."

"Then..."

"All three have got different fathers."

I hadn't realised this and it came as a bit of a shock.

"Can't the other father's help..."

"No, none of them want to help me. They are bastards all of them. All they wanted was to fuck me. After that they couldn't give a stuff."

"I see."

"I just can't help myself. You know, sometimes I've just got to have it. That's the way it is with me. Most of the time I couldn't care less for men, they are all a mob a prats anyway. But then sometimes I've just got to have them. You know how it is."

The youngest one started to cry for seemingly no apparent reason. Perhaps it was the desperation and anger in Sarah's voice that upset her, whatever it was Sarah diligently attended to her with comforting words.

I took the opportunity, whilst the passenger's attention was distracted, to turn off the meter.

The shopping centre taxi rank loomed and a sense of

excitement, emulated from the children. A new stimulus, visible human activity, noise, perchance to experience purchasing. The tears had dried.

Parked, the inside of the vehicle became active with the unbuckling of seat belts. Sarah passed me her bank card without looking to see how much the fare was. I hoped there might be enough left for a bag of lollies.

Billy and his Missus

In the centre of the main street there were two hotels next to each other. By their architecture they were possibly the first hotels in this town. At different stages the competition between the hotel owners would have been fierce. At other stages, as if playing the Monopoly board game, both hotels were owned jointly.

It took me a time to figure out which name was associated with which hotel. Billy aided me in this understanding.

It was a regular job, usually later in the afternoon. I had learnt that this pub was the first one of the duo and its name stuck as a result of the passenger.

He was always seated on the bench seat outside the hotel, waiting. He would see the taxi approaching before the driver had the indicator on.

He was a very small man, carrying no extra weight. His wrinkled face and slightly hunched back told of his advanced years. Yet his energetic walk belied his age. With enthusiasm and two long necks of beer he would enter always into the back seat.

Certainly fashion was not his interest. His clothes, obviously that had seen their fair share of toil bore the tale of a physicality in Billy's activities. But not your modern brightly coloured fluoro outfits as had become working man cultural uniform, but old fashioned attire that would've been used fifty years previous.

Although I had never met him completely sober it always was obvious to me that many of his day's hours had been spent at the bar. As a matter of routine in fact, and at this time, according to routine, it was time to go home.

Also, as a matter of routine, even before any words were spoken, a ten dollar note was thrust onto the driver.

We had built up a rapport with regards to communicating. It was really quite simple. He knew me enough to know that I was a good listener and as such I had no need to start a conversation. He would start it, without gaps for a reply. All that was needed was the occasional "Yes", "Really", and to praise his ego, which needed constant support, "You did really well, with that one, then."

"He sent me over to Mrs McIntyre's place this morning, up near the hospital. Give me that bloody old bloody lawn mower again. I keep telling him the thing is stuffed but he still gets me to use it. It wouldn't go, again so I had to pull the whole thing apart. Found what was the problem though. A block in the fuel line it was. Bit of crap was lodged in there, had to blow it out in the end, bloody well tasted foul."

"Well done," was another of my more used set of words for a reply.

"And he always leaves it too long to cut the lawn. I tell him it's not good for this old lawn mower to be doing such tough jobs, but do you reckon he listens to me. No he just smiles at me. And then when I've got all the parts over her lawn she comes out and tells me not to spill any fuel over her lawn. Bloody old biddie, how am I going to clear a fuel line without spilling any? I managed not to though, but gees it tasted horrible."

"You did really well with that one then."

"He paid me though this week, makes for a change, in cash of course. Not as much as I deserve. He'd be stuffed without me you know. The things I've done for him..."

His abode was on Tuckan Avenue, situated about half way along this thoroughfare. It was a fibro dwelling which was coated in what used to be a creamy colour. However it was logical to assume, by its current appearance that this creamy colour was the original colour covered decades previous. Its original creaminess had faded towards brown. A couple of roses bushes, which were refusing to flower even though it was late spring, adorned the pathway to the entrance. They seemed to be in conflict with the grasses that shared their space. The grasses, which populated amongst the lawn area, enjoyed a freedom of domination aided by the fact that it was allowed to flourish. The shin high wooden post and rail fence which stood as a border to the street, was obscured, most of the time, by grasses.

Yes, he might've lived in a rather undesirable section of this town but it was obvious that his tough, street wise existence had prepared him for such an environment. It was a given that he felt at ease in this setting.

Directly opposite his address there grew a group of melaleuca trees. So established were they that they hid the houses behind them. Enclave into the bottom branches a sort of cave had been evolved through years of human social occupation. It was a meeting place for the locals. Chairs backed into the branches and wheelie bins showed regular use. The varied and empty containers of alcoholic beverages that didn't make it into the wheelie bins stayed where they had been left.

Usually at this time of the afternoon persons had gathered to discuss the day's affairs. There were the usual's, those who lived in the hidden houses and others who would appear on occasions.

Billy's rave would end as I would park beside the Melaleuca trees. Whether the story had ended or not it would suddenly stop. His attention would be now drawn to a new audience.

The new audience would always greet him with affection as though their afternoon's attendance was now complete. They would also be very respectful of the taxi driver who bought their kin back to them. They were a happy crew, happy with their lot and comfortable in their existence as they discussed the current happenings in this town. The price of fuel at the service station in the main street as compared to the ones on the highway was discussed. Who that bloke in number is 56 is seeing. Whether Jack's missus was back with him again or still pissed off with him? When Connor's court case was coming up and other such important matters?

There was another regular passenger that would be taken to the same address. The pickup point was different though. The taxi rank at the shopping centre was the anointed place.

She would be sitting on the bench seats waiting for the taxi to arrive. When it did she would be ready for the journey home. It was always a given to help her with her load of groceries.

She would look at me with small beady intense eyes. At first I could never decipher if the intensity in her eyes were of suspicion, anxiety or just old age. There was little emotion displayed on her face, all seemed to be routine as a matter of course. Her hunched body, which seemed to have been deformed with age, would move slowly towards the backseat, clutching her handbag tightly.

It was given, with no words uttered, that I was responsible for the groceries. That task completed, I would find her set, with seat-belt on, for the journey home as I readied for the driving.

Similar to Billie, there was no need to start a conversation, her quiet and reserved demure, as portrayed on the waiting bench, now quickly dissipated. All I had to do was to select the correct response to the vocal stimuli.

However this was quite difficult. All I would hear from the back seat was a mumbled noise. It was extremely difficult to decipher what, in fact, she was saying.

From the first time I collected her, it troubled me that I could not understand a single word she said. Therefore I was always uncertain as to which response to give. Till one time, understanding the difficulty in communication, I watched her talking before the taxi became in motion. It revealed to me that the poor lady had no teeth, her tongue had been depleted through some previous ailment and that this was why her language was in decipherable. Her physical attributes for talking had been severely depleted. Hence all she could do now to aid in her communicative processes was to mumble.

Of course the mumble would sometimes become quite intense. This would evoke a "Really" response from me. With, of course, the appropriate, compassionate empathy. Hoping it was correct response for the tale being told.

Sometimes, however, by the sudden pause in the noise from the back seat, I worried that I had said the wrong response. My anxiety would be curtailed with the continuation of the muffled words of no understanding. I wondered upon the subject matter of her dialogue as though I had missed out on something. I was never going to find out since her tales would always be a mystery caused by her lack of speech.

As with Billie the chatter, or noise, would end abruptly when the taxi stopped into her driveway. It was the usual cause of events. The passion and determined delivery of her oracle faded as a new stimuli presented itself.

The passage up the footpath to the door was always an arduous process for her. I wondered if it was not a combination of resignation to the end of her outing, or just old age, or disappointment that she could not be understood. I would place the groceries next to her door and wondered how she would get them into the house and stored away. I took restoration in the fact that she showed a toughness borne from the years of a struggled life.

Perhaps when Billie returned home, after the two long necks and whatever else presented itself, that she might find someone that could decipher her mumbling.

Chris, part 2

The camaraderie amongst my fellow taxi drivers was very evident. We were all in the same boat, waiting for fares. The conversations usually revolved around just that, waiting for fares. Occasionally the talk would be centred on a difficult or interesting client. It was good to have people to relate these incidents to as there was no one else interested. Lest of all the clients who were usually too full of their own lives, in their sheltered trails, to be in the least concerned about the driver. We were but mirrors to their own predicaments without any physicality or soul. One found oneself drifting into a certain narrow minded space, much like our clients were in, that revolved around either waiting for fares, listening to client's problems and watching out for other drivers.

At shifts end the now usual retreat to my apartment, with its walls to keep the day's exchanges on the outside. There was no one to talk to, in this space. I tried taking myself down to one of the hotels on different occasions, perchance someone to talk to. But I knew no one and thus a stranger I remained. I resigned myself to the safety of my own structured cave, solitude again. But something was missing.

The staff, who worked at the office, was rarely encountered. Shifts started and finished at hours that were not conducive to the regular office hours. Often the only people seen each day were the other drivers, the clients and the faked faces on the television in my abode.

It was a Thursday morning and a very typical day where clients needed to be at specific places at certain times. Not least of all mothers wanting to drop off their pre-schoolers to leave them with a free day.

Such a call came and for shame there was not a child's seat in the sedan I was assigned to. With haste a return to base where I knew there were plenty. They were stored at the back of this house come small single business centre. To save time in backing out of the narrow driveway I parked on the street. It was quicker to walk to the back of the house. Hurriedly I entered the driveway. I sighted Chris, the administrator, working along the driveway, whipper-sniper in hand, mowing down the weeds that flourished during the spring. I was surprised to see her as our paths seldom met, especially with a machine under her control.

She noticed my hastened approach. She smiled a genuine smile which led me to believe there was a genuine interest in this particular taxi driver.

"Forgotten something?" She said.

"Child's seat."

"They are in that..."

"Yeah, I know where they are, thanks."

Although I was in a hurry her friendliness warranted further converse. My curiosity overpowered my urgency. I paused my walking.

"Multi skilled?" Referring to her current task.

"He pays me cash for doing this, it all helps, you know. I'll be finished this soon, then go inside and do what I normally do."

"Then back again tomorrow."

"Oh no, I only work here two days a week."

"Do you have another job?"

"No, I can't. I'm only allowed to earn so much before it affects what I earn for looking after my parents. There's so much to do on the farm and looking after mum and dad, I nearly don't have enough time for this but I have to."

I wanted to ask more but the urgency of the job prevented me. The encounter had left me with still more questions about this lady that needed answering.

Perchance our paths met on other occasions leading up to Christmas. Always in a rush but always a very friendly greeting and a longing to have more of a "get to know you better," chat.

Christmas day happens even for taxi drivers. Many of the drivers had families which demanded their involvement. I had no such commitments thus I manned the taxi ranks for some days. It was noticeable that the newer bridge, the one that conveyed the through traffic, was much busier than the old bridge. Not only by the increased through traffic being holidays but for the fact that many of this town's inhabitants had gone away. It was a very quiet time to be driving taxis.

Boredom had set in by the middle of the day when suddenly my phone rang. It surprised me and awoken me from the tedium. Chris's voice was recognisable.

"Scott, sorry to disturb you..."

"It's all right, I'm not doing much."

"I've left the keys of the office inside and I need to get some stuff. When you get a chance I was wondering if you could come and open up the back door, please."

Not currently doing much and in need of something different, I replied, "Sure."

There was another driver on who was out on a call, so I turned my switchboard onto "coffee cup", which signified unavailability. I found Chris at the back of the house waiting patiently. She looked relieved when I appeared.

"I'm really sorry about this," she started.

"It's all right, it's broken the boredom."

The back door was accessible by keys. I found mine and utilised it.

"Thank you so much." Whereby she entered without hesitation as though she had other things to do and this complication was a nuisance.

My task done, at this point I could've left but my curiosity towards this woman kept me for her return.

She did return, stuff in hand, much more relieved. Post Christmas, there was always only one conversation starter.

"So how did you spend Christmas?" I asked.

She sensed the genuine in my delivery. It was more than a conversation starter. She was surprised that I seemed interested and seemed keen to have a chat.

"I didn't do much, cooked the lunch for mum and dad. They were happy with it. In the afternoon they went to sleep which meant I could spend time with my horse."

"You didn't have more family with you?"

A seemingly simple question in a logical progression was met with a reaction that I was not expecting. It was as though I had unwittingly made a faux pas. My question had pressed a sensitive nerve that was still in pain.

"So what did you do?" Her "change of topic" response confirmed my impression.

"I worked."

"Don't you have a family?"

"No."

She looked at me with great surprise as though it was not the response she was expecting. Her face moved to sympathetic mode.

"Mum died seventeen years ago. I was her only child. I never knew my father," I continued.

Wanting to change the topic, I asked, "So, did you get up to much socialising with your friends. It's what you do at Christmas, isn't it?"

She paused before replying, "I don't really have a lot of friends, we keep to our selves. Besides I always have so much to do."

At this moment we both realised, although our situations were different, we both suffered the same ailment, loneliness. With that shared vibe I felt our relationship become suddenly stronger. Maybe there was now a mutual need towards each other. An embarrassed loll occurred in the dialogue. I thought of maybe asking her out for a drink or something but was hesitant that it might be seen to be too forward, too early. Perhaps I deemed it to be inappropriate or perhaps I was just too shy.

The silence was broken when she stated, "Well I better get this stuff back to mum, she's waiting for it."

End result, I didn't. Besides she now knew my phone number.

Mitchell

The first week of January and the post Christmas blues were setting in. Gone was the enthusiasm of the run up to Christmas and its expectations. The excess of parties had worn themselves into a continuous hang over. The conversations had dried to repeats. The novelty of continuous days off had in itself become a tedious bore of family diplomacy.

Saturday morning, the sun was rising in a usual fashion for summer, instantly stamping its heat upon the scene. The shift was just starting as the rays of light hit the taller trees, filtering down to the now very familiar road around to the taxi stand.

The town seemed tired from too much frivolity. The inhabitants had long gone to slumber not looking forward to this day's nausea.

Parked in the bay, not expecting much, perhaps there was something interesting on the radio. But even the announcer lacked enthusiasm, suffering the same malaise as the listeners. The day, at this stage, appeared to be uninspiring.

Resigned to the semi slumber of the radio noise I entered into that bored state.

Without warning, as it usually does, and as to awaken me from the motionless present, the sound of a job blasted into my unprepared ears. There was something to do, a different experience to be attained.

Taxi into go mode, the address was a park near the highway

very near to a couple of more notorious hotels. At night one might fell a tingle of anxiety, wondering what drunken mind was about to enter. But since the sun was letting forward it's full force of restricting qualities, I felt safer.

The park was surrounded by four different roads. Which one would lead to the clients was a guess. I chose the one closest to the hotels. I was right.

Two men stood in the park under a tree. I saw them before they saw me. I parked the taxi closest as I could to them on the left with the park across the road, and waited. Surely, since they would've been waiting for the taxi and one had arrived I shouldn't have to wait too long.

Not so. I looked over towards them to investigate the hesitation. The two men were obviously in some sort of confrontation, too absorbed into the personal relationship to have noticed the reason for their presence in this place, at this time.

By their slurred movements, almost bordering upon staggers, I assumed they had had a long night of intoxication. A dreading thought enter my psyche. Perhaps a short beep of the horn might awaken them to their current, more realistic, purpose.

It did and they were bought out of that time warp. Forgetting their previous discussion, they hurried across to the taxi. I thought it was only for one passenger. Was I now to be lumbered with two potentially conflicting clients?

Fortunately, as they approached I could study their details more closely. The bigger man, with fairer hair, seemed to be more in control of his functions. The other smaller man with short black hair, a little receding, tailed behind the other man. He was obviously suffering from the night more that the fair haired one.

"You the one taking Mitchell home to the heights?" The

bigger one asked hoping I was his saviour to release him from this current human bond.

"Yes," I replied. To which he open the back door, facing the road.

Mitchell, by now, had caught up. He looked a little bewildered. Confused by what was now expected of him. His mate beckoned him towards the opened door. He stood a little too far out onto the road to really feel safe, and still looked with little understanding.

"Just get into the car, will ya?" his mate ordered in such a tone that a respond had to ensue. It did and an uncoordinated bundle of flesh seemed to ooze into the space the back seat provided.

"Just get him home will ya mate? I've had enough of him."

Mitchell's mate had enough care left in him to get a seat belt around Mitchell in some sort of fashion. Then he reached into his pocket and handed me a twenty dollar note.

"That should be enough to get him home."

Fortunately I knew the address I had to go to, I had been there before. I hoped the body in the back seat would not make a nuisance of himself. The taxi was in motion.

Soon after, before we had gotten to the intersection of the highway a noise emerged from the back seat. It was a voice that exhumed a severe lack in confidence. It was a weak voice seemingly crying out for help, the voice of a little boy trying to make sense of a world in chaos. Except he was not a little boy, he was a young man in his late twenties. One who should've been a lot more together than what the noise from the back seat was projecting.

I was trying, although I didn't really want to, decipher if the mumbled noise from the back seat was actually trying to articulate words.

I listened carefully to make sense of the oratory in case a reply was necessary. After careful study of the different style of diction, and the cyclical nature of the sounds, repeated without cessation, I began to understand a bit of the vocabulary being used.

"She's going to kill me," seemed to be a predominate statement.

This collection of words in this same order continued as I made my way up the highway. It got to the point that I began to toil with the idea that a reply might be, in fact, necessary. I initially believed that the dialogue from the backseat was purely personal, like one thinking aloud, but my doubts on this scenario had weakened.

"Who's going to kill you?" I asked politely.

I was surprised to realise that he actually heard my response. With greater impudence he expressed.

"She's going to kill me."

I could sense a certain cyclical nature developing into our conversation, excepting that I could sense a real fear, worry and general concern in his last response.

I knew this address. It was a series of six very small flats fitted into a normal suburban house block. They looked small and cramped. It was to be hoped that the rent was cheap as they did not look very appealing as a home sweet home. As a result of a few visits to this address I had concluded that the rentals were cheaper as evident by the inhabitants.

Several weeks earlier I picked up a passenger from the hospital to be taken to this same address. (I had an inkling upon who the "she" was). She was waiting for me in the emergency car park of the hospital. She didn't look well upon first appearances. Her hunched body, coughing lungs, and tangled, once possibly pretty but now faded and dirty looking hair, gave the appearance of one who should've been staying in hospital.

She was pleased to see the taxi arrive as if this heralded an escape from an environment she did not wish to be involved in. She would've been in her late thirties although her present appearance suggested older. She showed evidence of a "racey" life of trying anything and now showing the scars of too many "out of it" experiences.

Her breath was obviously short as she clambered into the back seat.

She told me the address but asked if I could drop into the servo to get a packet of cigarettes. She seemed pleased to be going home.

"Did they fix you up?" I asked trying to be positive.

"They can't do anything for me. I've got emphysema from too much smoking. They reckon I've only got months to go."

Her news sent me silent in shock.

"They reckon they can't do anything for me but send me home and keep me monitored."

Her dialogue was suddenly interrupted by an intense cough.

"And stay away from people, they said. All to do with this COVID stuff that's going on. Stuff that, I want to go out. I haven't got long to go so why not have a good time."

The servo loomed and I indicated to enter it. Parked, her door opened.

"I won't be long."

In sympathy I placed the meter on "pause". Sometimes kindness must over ride convention. It is what makes us human.

She returned promptly with two different brands of smokes. This stimulated my curiosity.

"Why two brands?"

"One for this drop kick of a bloke I've got living with me at the moment. He's always running out of smokes."

"It's good that you have someone there to look after you."

"Who's looking after who? I'm the one that's looking after him. You wait, when I get home he won't have done any cleaning, he'll have barely had any food. I'll have to feed him and tidy the place up a bit, and when I want to go out tonight he'll come up with some excuse until his mates come around and pick him up. Then he'll want to go out. Bloody hell, stuff that. If he pulls that one on me again, I'm going out with my mates. I'm going to have a good time, anyway."

In my role at this time I always felt it important to be purely objective, not to give any moral or subjective opinions. I was to be almost as a councillor, a set of ears to a dialogue without a voice. However this time I couldn't resist in stating the obvious.

"Why do you put up with it?"

"Because he's got no one else. He's hopeless, no job, no prospects, nowhere to live, no desire to live. Who else is going to look after him?"

The continued cyclic nature of Mitchell's conversation with himself was beginning to press the irritation button. Let's turn a negative into a positive with knowledge upon who "she" was.

"Perhaps, when you get home, you could make her a cup of coffee?"

"I don't know how to."

It is sometimes difficult to be positive when the subject is determined to stay in the negative. But one must try.

"Tell her how much you love her, that might help."

"It's a bit hard to tell someone you love them when they are blowing you up all the time."

"You do love her?"

"I can't live without her."

"Then care for her no matter what she's on about, that will show your love for her is greater than the conflict."

The address loomed, the bundle of incoherent mess in the back seat realised the impending doom as the car slowed to a stop.

Perhaps the rest in the back seat had created a bit of initiative as Mitchell seemed capable of undoing the seat belt.

Silently he emerged from the car banging the door as he departed. The mutterings of "She's going to kill me" continued as he walked towards the door of their flat.

My job done, I didn't wait around to witness the consequences.

It did turn out to be a rather slow day until later in the afternoon. The few jobs that came on offer presented passengers that were tired of the idle chit chat but rather resigned themselves to a quiet afternoon going home to do very little.

By three thirty, however, the tempo had picked up. Hungry for another night out amidst this festive season with an end they filed once more in an effort to ease their hangovers.

No sooner had one job finished when another one presented itself. The waiting time was increasing. Another booking in this rush appeared. A glance at the address revealed itself to be the address I had taken Mitchell to in the morning. This fare had been waiting for some time. Urgency prevailed.

Curious to discover the outcome of this morning drama, I made my way to the said address. I pulled into the narrow driveway, uniform to all of the little cars stationed in small car parks adjacent to their little flats.

To my surprised all the residents of the little flats were all out of their abodes, in the bright sunshine, each showing signs of a drama, distress, a trauma that had just happened. The atmosphere was very tense as I waited for the fare to appear.

My appearance had not gone unnoticed. Amidst the confused interaction of humans recounting with the dramatic consequences, a charismatic man advanced towards me. He realised that I did not know the current situation and wanted to enlighten me. His face was quite concerned as I winded down my window to hear what he had to say.

"Are you here for flat one?"

"Yes."

"They won't be needing you now. She's just been taken to hospital with blood coming from her ears and the police have just taken him away."

Paul, part 2

Summer had peaked but the high temperatures still lingered. The taxi's air conditioning was being put to good use. Late January, the first hint of the shortening days, the enthusiasm of the holidays was well past. Looming was the congeniality of work and financial commitments.

Approaching lunch time and a call came from Paul's address. I had been driving for the company for long enough to have built up a rapport with the regulars. Paul was not an exception, to the point where I looked forward to his company. There was always a laugh in store.

When I arrived the thought was reciprocated when he saw that it was me. He felt comfortable enough with me to sit in the front seat, despite any restrictions.

"Lunch time?" I said as he made himself comfortable. He looked at me with his bright, appealing blue eyes, and in a tone to state, "obviously" he replied politely with a certain dryness,

"Yes please."

"Important meetings today in the office, is it? Million dollar deals to be nutted out?" I asked with a dry humour which was accustomed to our conversations.

"No, I'm just discussing the human condition with three schooners of beer. I'll leave the deals to the wife. She good at those sort of things."

I hadn't seen him since before Christmas. It was usually a

conversation piece.

"So how did you spend Christmas?"

"I got trapped, didn't I."

"How?"

"The wife wanted to go visit her family didn't she?"

"Where was that?"

"You heard of a place called Ivanhoe?"

"Yes. Out the back of New South Wales."

"That's it."

"Not much there."

"Even less where her folks live."

"Have a good time?"

"I was bored shitless. There's nothing to do out there. Hanging around in the heat. Putting up with an endless array of flies."

"Friendly were they?"

"The flies?"

He didn't wait for my reply.

"Really friendly. All wanted to become intimate with me, buggers of things. Then there were the sheep. They had me out mustering one day, in the heat, the flies and the dust, somewhere in the middle of nowhere. No pubs for miles. I was not well entertained that day. She was born to it, I wasn't. I would've rather to be sitting at the MCG watching the cricket with me mates, over a couple of glasses of beer in the members."

"You must've enjoyed being with her folks?"

"No. They all go for Collingwood. What's more Collingwood beat us the last time we met. I didn't broach the topic."

Waiting at the set of lights which seemed constantly to be red whenever I approached them from whatever direction, I pondered.

"So did you get to see the cricket?"

"No they don't like the game. Terribly uncultured mob they are. It is just not the done thing to organise a big sheep day on boxing day. On boxing day civilised people comfort themselves in front of the television to watch the first ball of the day. Instead I'm in some set of yards hunting these silly bloody sheep down a race, choking from the dust, the flies, the heat, the smell and the yapping dogs. Not my idea of what boxing day should be."

At last the lights changed and the pub loomed.

"So did you see any of the day's play?"

"No."

"Probably just as well, we were all out for not much on that day."

"Yeah well, I would've liked to have seen how we were out for not much. I had to sneak out to the car to catch up on the scores and that was if I was lucky. Not much radio reception out there. Plenty of flies though."

The destination was arrived at. The bar was calling him. He fumbled through his pockets to find a note. Without looking at the meter he handed me a twenty dollar note which was much more than the fare.

"Keep the change."

"Thanks Mate. Tell me if your three beers can answer any questions upon what we are all doing here, will ya?"

"They wouldn't know. Best not to wonder about that. Just exist and enjoy three the beers. Safer that way."

As he departed into the confines of the licensed premises I

wondered about his wife that he spoke so much of. I had never seen or met her and I was curious upon what she and their relationship was really like.

Clare

A call came to an address that I was now familiar with. It was a little house at the back of a close with the railway line outside the back door.

Although the address was familiar it was never certain as to who was being picked up. The names on the screen changed so rapidly it was hard to keep up with them. Let alone a face to a name.

I had deduced that it was a three bedroom house. Given the size of the house they were three very small bedrooms. Each room must've housed a couple. As for the pairings I could never make it out as the faces changed rapidly.

It was a shared house amongst couples. Each was at that restless stage of their lives, the early twenties, when the excitement of youth still commanded attention but the possibilities were giving way to practicalities. Decisions being made as to which direction their lives will lead them. Yet a night out, having a good time was never out of the question. Each of them was searching for that missing thread that will lead them into that cycle of conformity, when life becomes a secure habit of mundanely. It helps them to pass the time when the career takes over from the raging. But at this stage, the early twenties, life still held its adventure. Swapping jobs, finding new avenues, trying to find some sense of the confusion called living.

At this time they should've been out raging. But not so for quite a few months now as the COVID lockdown had had a dramatic effect on their social life.

Unsure as to which face I was going to be greeted with, I didn't have to wait long, the blonde hair and girlish walk made Clare easily recognisable. Mask securely attached she hurried down the path as though she had been waiting for me. A sure sign that work was beckoning.

She greeted me with her customary happy, smiling face but this time showed the signs of a bit of stress. As though there was something troubling her which the taxi driver was not to be privy to. This was no exception.

I received the usual destination information although it was not necessary I had taken her to work before. She worked in a retirement village. The job for her was still relatively new. She was still learning the procedures.

The usual process of usual conversation pieces about the weather and other trivial subjects ensued until I tried to be a little personal.

"How are you finding your new job?"

A pause in the conversation commenced, I wondered if I had hit a wrong note in conversation. The reply answered my question. I was in the right key.

"I'm a bit worried about it. I mean, like, I can do the job and, like, they are all really good but, like I wear the mask all the time, as they all do there, but, like, I haven't had my second Vaccination for the COVID virus and I should've had it to be working where I am. I'm really worried about it all."

"How come you haven' t had it?"

"There's nowhere to get it in this town. You can only get it in the next town, down the railway track, like. I haven't got a car and you can't travel by public transport."

"Are you feeling all right?"

"Like yes, but, you know there are a few cases getting about the town now and like they are making all this fuss about the retirement villages on the news and like, you know, what if I bring it into the village."

"Do they know this at work?"

"Yes, I've told them. They reckon someone's going to come into the village and give us all the vaccination, but like, when? They're so short of staff you see and like, you know, they need me there. And like, I can't afford not to be there. We've still got to pay the rent, pay the bills and like we're trying to save money for a house. All of us in that house are in the same position. Jose works behind a bar, how many people does she come into contact with? She's really good though, always has her mask on even at home. We all do."

"Stay healthy then and don't go out."

"I know. We don't go anywhere any more. One of us goes and gets the groceries and that's it. We can't go anywhere, not even to other towns. None of us want to get sick and especially as they all know where I work. I'm like really worried about it all. And like, when will it all end?"

The Public Servant

It came the time of the year to renew the registration of my vehicle. Late summer was starting to take its effect. A southerly had blown up after a storm the previous evening. The sudden change of temperature had caught the inhabitants of this small country town by surprise. They cuddled into their rediscovered winter garments.

The COVID situation was in panic mode as dictated to by the authorities. Sometimes, though, the people didn't always follow the directives.

Car parked, now began the task of assembling all the paper work and documents needed for such bureaucracy to be processed. Slips of paper collected, wallet included, keys in my hand, it was time to feel the shock of this new climate.

It did come as a shock. The door to the building housing the appropriate group of public servants loomed. The thought of a warmer environment inside served as a satisfactory motivator to exit the street and its nasty wind, quickly.

A young man guarded the entrance. He looked like a junior in this organisation. He showed the enthusiasm belonging to a new beckoning career. He seemed to be the guardian of the precinct. He was the man of authority with power. Each person that approached the entrance was being inspected by him before safe passage into the warmth indoors could be obtained. He kept his stern brow as though to indicate that he demanded attention. His face was hidden behind a mask. This seemed to aid in his quest for authority as his subjects had difficulty properly reading his facial expressions. Thus, uncertainty leads to fear where a directive is instantly obeyed.

He was clad in a thick coat which hid his shape to a certain extent. However it was quite obvious he was not the sporty type, rather he had spent his exercise going to the local fast food depot. His weight was a little excessive. He might not have been able to score a try on the rugby field but he knew his bulk could stop access to anyone.

My progress towards his sanctum was drawing to a conclusion. I was now within his jurisdiction.

His eyes fixed firmly upon me. He was sussing me out. Then I could read, by his limited body movements, that a conversation was going to ensue. I could see his eyes and they seemed to narrow with his thought upon my case. He even started to approach me before I'd arrived at his position. I figured he really had something urgent to say to me. I also figured I was going to be subjected to his authority.

He spoke to me in a tone that was bordering upon frustration and fanaticism. However, since he had a mask over his face I found it very difficult to understand anything that he was saying. It was obvious that he had something very earnest to say to me. The urgency in his tone was apparent. His diligence in performing his task to the best of his ability was evident. But I still couldn't really understand a word he was saying. His dictation was so fast and with such passion that the auditory became confused due to the impediment of his mask.

I stood there trying to ascertain what this tyrant was about as he became increasingly angry with me for not complying.

Trying to appease his directives I suggested.

"Mate, I'd love to do as you want, but I can't understand a word you're saying."

He stood for a moment in silence which could be interrupted as either him trying to understand what I'd just said, deciding whether I was a threat to his authority or whether he should think of another way to communicate to this human who had just spoken to him.

The latter proved to be the most effective. His silence continued but his hands did not. He moved them to his mask. I thought for a moment he was going to take it off so as I could understand what he was saying but no, the silence continued. Rather, he placed his hands under the bottom side of his mask, pulled at it and pointed to me.

He had communicated. I suddenly realised, much to my embarrassment, that I hadn't bought with me my mask. I had been too preoccupied with the correct paperwork for this bureaucratic process that I'd forgotten an essential item of one's attire in this era.

In keeping with his cue of communicating I remained silent but also pointed to my face as if to transfer to him that I understood what he was trying to say.

He indicated with a favourable vibe that he was confident that I knew what he was on about.

I navigated a different direction. It was completely opposite to the former one. In fact it was quite reversed. I turned and headed back towards my car. Feeling embarrassed and also loathing that I had to endure more of this biting wind.

This return journey was notably different in that it was much quicker. It didn't take long to find the now essential apparatus. Paper work still in hand and mask placed between my fingers, car locked, I made my way back to the little man's domain.

I was again approaching him and he chanced to stare at my progress. In order to comply with his directives and to prove such I made a point of placing my mask, correctly, over my face.

I hoped that this action would satisfy his demands. I felt confident that it would and the warmth of the building would be granted to me.

His expression was still stern. To the point where I wondered if I had done something else wrong. Unfortunately there was no one else approaching which meant he could pay his full attention to me. It was obvious that I was to be targeted. To emphasis the strategy he even moved so as to inhibit my path. I was stopped. A lamb, that was being stared at by a lion.

His first line of fire in this battle was noise. I was convinced that it did emulate from his throat via a voice box and tongue, however the impediment of his mask still proved to be a huge problem. I couldn't understand a word he was saying, again. I stood as subserviently as I could so as to register to him my obedience to whatever he was saying. I even considered bowing, like they did in Japan, wondering if that would work. I dismissed that idea though realising he might not have known about the custom in a foreign land. Still the enthusiastic and very passionate mumbling still projected forthwith.

I tried to guess what he might have been on about. It would not have been about the local football team or perhaps it was about what he had for dinner the previous evening. Or was it about the changing weather. I tendered to doubt these explanations as the diligence in his noise suggested something of much more importance. I felt that I had complied with all of his wishes. Was I not now acting the subservient role? Why still this entourage of power? Perhaps I was being given a lecture upon the importance of masks so as he could exercise his power of this human. Like a little child who was now given the authority to assert himself. I couldn't tell.

I became bored of my cynicism and this charade had gone on for long enough. He was testing my Buddhist inspired tolerance.

Fortunately, I caught out of the corner of my eye, without losing his attention, some people approaching the building. This was my best chance of escape. Subtly I looked at the people. At first he might have been a little offended that I was not paying him my full attention. But when he saw the new players, our conflict was concluded.

With his gaze distracted, I slipped in to the warmth of the building. I left the boy with a new set of companions with which to play his game.

Chris, part 3

Summer had now become a memory. The vibrancy of the December sun had lost its enthusiasm. Jumpers were on constant standby. The excitement of a new year had given way to the conformity of yet another day at work.

My fellow taxi drivers had once again fallen into the mundanely of the usual fares. Five minute chats before being broken by necessity, never revelling much at all. We lived in a cave called a driver's seat and never to weaken our vocational walls. Conversational topics were always centred around the current situation and never about what happens after the shift. I was learning more about them than they were about me. My life was hidden from them. I was hoping for something closer.

Back at base after the shift when there was a chance to relax and confide, maybe find someone to relate to. However they were in too much of a hurry to return to their own walled abodes, like the passengers they had picked up during the day, to be ready for the next day's set of fares. Our private lives were sheltered and hidden.

Occasionally staff members were still at base when a shift ended. Usually to be waiting for someone from the shift to fulfil some directive.

Chris was the most visible of the staff since she was the one involved in the bureaucracy of it all. Her presence provided a pleasant interaction to the drivers. She was always very welcoming and understanding to them. Maybe it was her naturally likeable nature or was it her longevity in the job? Whatever it was the drivers could relate to her easily.

She would ask the driver about their day. It was usually met with a talkative response. Such a good listener was she that the responsive answer would often divulge information that was not necessarily required.

It was noticeable to me that, during her interactions with the driver's none of them would ask her about her day or indeed her circumstances. She would always maintain her professional distance. To the drivers and I she was an enigma. There would always remain many unanswered questions, never to be asked of her.

The sun had set and the chill was creeping into the countryside. I was warm in the taxi, coming back from an out of town call. There was good money in those. My mood was high and I was looking forward to knocking off. I wasted no time to transverse the kilometres as I also knew a night shift driver would be waiting for this vehicle.

The headlights of the taxi revealed his shadowy figure as I entered the driveway. It seemed to move with relief upon my appearance.

As I turned into the parking area behind the house/office I could see another figure. The feeble back light of the building cast a little clarity onto the scene. By the slim figure and distinctive hair, it was obviously Chris. I wondered what had kept her out in the cold at this time of day.

Forms filled out Norm, the night shift driver, wasted no time in being operational. That left Chris and I.

"He's in a bit of a hurry because he's got a call to one of the mines to take someone to the airport." Chris explained.

"I got here as soon as I could."

"Oh, we knew that. In actual fact you got here quicker than we expected."

"You doing the night shift too?" I asked dryly.

"Oh no, I've been waiting for you as well. You're a popular person this evening."

I learned that there was yet another bureaucratic procedure to be undertaken. We progressed into her room/office and fulfilled the necessary requirements.

With the necessities accomplished she started the conversation remembering our previous chat. (We didn't encounter much of each other and she did well to recount my situation.)

"So how are you finding our little town?"

"It's all right, I suppose. I don't go out very much so the people I work with are really the only ones that I know."

She paused as if this was not the response she was expecting. Then, as if our memories had registered to the same thought at the same time, we remembered our conversation post Christmas. The moment when we both realised how inwardly lonely we both were.

An awkward silence commenced. Either we wanted to delve deeper and explore this commonality. Perhaps become closer and supportive of our predicament. Or move on as if that uniting thought did not exist. The answer was not of my making.

"Do you like where ....."

I could see where she was leading. The latter was to be the path. I was more interested in listening. I interrupted her.

"How are things on your property?"

She was taken by surprise and paused for a bit. Normally it was the drivers that would set upon a lengthy explanation to her with confidence. Suddenly the pattern was broken. In her eyes she seemed surprised that someone was actually interested in her circumstances.

She looked at me with surprise and a renewed respect. I think she might have even been flattered. I hoped that she may have realised that I really wanted to know more about her. It was as if, at first, she wanted to give a non informative response and change the topic but the pause indicated a change of attitude.

To help enforce my interest I asked, "Have you got any events lined up for your horse?"

In the dim light I could see her eyes light up as I had obviously chosen the right topic to loosen her walls.

"I'm hoping to take him to an event in a couple of weeks ......"

I listened intently and by her continued dialogue she could obviously tell the truth of my interest. To my surprise she continued for quite some time until a sudden zephyr of chilled air entered our space. It awoke her from the pleasant cognitive journey through her passion.

"Speaking of which I better get going and check him. I told Dad that I would be late home and he said he'd bed him down but you never know, Dad sometimes forget things."

I could sense her urgency as though the spell had now been broken.

"It's been nice talking to you Scott."

With which we both headed off to our different abodes.

Nigel

I learned that there was certainly a disparity between doing a day shift and a night shift.

The COVID restrictions had been lifted unexpectedly and the night shift was understaffed. Not enough drivers. Desperate situation needed an easy fix.

I had done the odd "over time" journey into the earlier hours of the night, but never a full gig. I was about to find out.

"I wonder if Scott might be able to fill in, we're got enough for the day shift, it's the night shift we need him for. He's already done part of the night shift." suggested the frustrated owner of the taxis, Bob, to his night shift supervisor Nick.

"Could he handle himself with a bad one. We get them at night?"

"Don't know,"

"He seems rather passive, how's he going to ...."

"He'll just have to we have no other choice."

The main disparity being that during the day time the clients were basically sober, conducting their normal day by day chores. At night their behaviour notably changes. I had experienced life enough to have gained a workable knowledge of people under the influence of alcohol. What I was not prepared for was a new toy called "Ice".

The night had been rather hectic. Not enough drivers and too many people out and about enjoying their sudden freedom. The jobs had been tallying up. A call came from a Nigel at one of the more "colourful" hotels, positioned on the highway. It was 11pm and he had ordered the taxi forty minutes earlier.

I pulled up, in a maxi taxi, on the other side of the highway to the hotel. It had dull lighting on the outside of the hotel,as if to try and hide its darker secrets. There were people scattered on the pavement, outside the hotel, with no continuity of social etiquette. Their noise and constant loud movements suggested a raucous behaviour that I didn't want to be involved in. The arrival of the taxi had drawn some attention. Curious eyes were set upon it. I was pleased I was on the other side of the highway.

Not wanting to draw attention to myself, or in particular the taxi, I searched for Nigel. Much movement amongst the groups on the pavement kept me focused upon which of these stumbling bodies would be Nigel venturing out to cross the highway.

I was suddenly surprised to hear the door of the maxi taxi give a confused noise as if trying to obey a muffled directive. I turned with alarm to see a body outside the door struggling not only to open the door but also to actually stand upright.

The surprise and the paranoia I had been suffering watching the mob on the pavement, instantly put me on alarm. I wasn't sure that this human, trying to open the door was, in fact, Nigel, or some lout trying to snare a taxi.

I pressed the button to open the passenger's window. I called out to the uncoordinated bundle of flesh, confused upon the operations of the door handle.

"Are you Nigel?"

A disjointed and obscured sound came from the figure which assured me that this person was, in fact, Nigel. The voice displayed a certain amount of anxiety. He was still trying to open the door with urgency. I contemplated whether I would have to disembark my driver's position in assistance. However to my relief I heard the door finally understand the uncertain signals from Nigel.

I looked across to a face that showed considerable discomfort. Either by his situation or, as I now discovered, a bloodied cheek bone. He was small and rather weedy in appearance. His clothes were tacky as if no thought had gone into trying to make himself appear presentable. He bore the face, bloodied as it was, of a trouble life of uncertainty and insecurity. He appeared as a lost sheep trying to make sense of it all. To nail an age to this individual was difficult to ascertain as he possibly looked older than what he was. A life spent inflicting self abuse had taken its toll.

As he struggled to get into the van I enquired about his injury.

"Some bloke just came up to me and slopped me."

Laterally speaking, was this action the effect or the cause? It had seemed to me, from our short acquaintance, that he would not be the assertive, aggressive type. Quite the opposite, one needs some sort of ego and self confidence to do this. He had none of these. With his drab black hair, darker clothes and very slight build, he would not be the one to stand out in a crowd; rather he would be hiding in a corner. Charisma was not his thing. The question beckoned.

"Why?" I inquired.

"I don't know. I was just sitting there and this crazy came up to me accusing me of stuff I didn't even know about, then he hit me."

I was in a quandary upon what was the truth, but his inability to secure himself into the seat let alone close the door and fasten his seat belt, took precedence. Anxious to escape this scene in case this mad person might be still seeking his victim, I suggested some ideas that might help.

"Close the door will you, mate?" Hoping he would understand me. He didn't, however he had by now found out how to be seated.

Still wanting to exit this place I pressed the point.

"Close the door will ya mate?"

"How does this seat belt work?" was his reply.

I now lost all hope that this person, whose mind had gone into blank, was going to fulfil these tasks. I quickly looked about the van to see if there were any undesirables about. There weren't and the people on the pavement had lost interest in the taxi.

I ventured out of the driver's seat and around to the still opened door. I advanced inside the van to assist this person who was suffering such a difficult passage. Managing to connect the two pieces of the apparatus that constitute the fastening of the seat belt I felt content that this person was now secure and that my obligations had been completed. I closed the door and resumed my place at the driver's position.

"Where are we going, mate?" I inquired.

"We've got to pick up my nephew."

Confused by this reply I was concerned that it was not totally the answer that I was seeking. His obscure reply led me to have doubts upon this fellow's current state of mind. He had suffered a blow to his head and I wondered if this had affected him.

"Do you think you need to go to the hospital?" I asked, conscious of his injury.

"No, I'm all right," was his reply which led me to doubt the authenticity of his words. However these were the client's directives and needed to be obeyed.

"Where's your nephew?" I asked with the motor now running and willing to exit this scene.

"I don't know," was the reply I didn't want to hear.

"So where am I taking you?"

"Home,"

Another reply that was of little use.

As diplomatically as I could, in order to hide my frustration and my anxiety to get away from this place, I replied, "Where's that?"

"Birrell street, in the heights, but we've got to find my nephew."

"So where might he be?"

The engine was still running and anxious to move but the direction was still in doubt. The heights were, in fact, behind me and a U turn of some description was necessary. Which might not be the easiest obstacle to encounter as this was the perpetual moving highway. However the quandary over the nephew left me a little directionless.

"Somewhere between here and home. He left a bit ago, said he was going home, that's when I ordered the taxi. I'm supposed to be looking after him. He's me brother's son down from Queensland, he wants to get work in the mines here and I'm supposed to be looking after him."

His semi coherent rave gave me confidence that he could actually articulate, very handy in these situations and gave me confidence that a trip to the hospital wasn't that necessary. At least I now knew which direction I was to head. I wasted no time in placing the gearbox into drive, indicators on and pulled out.

"You're going the wrong way," was the advice I received from the body in the seat behind me.

"Yeah I know, but I'm going to do a U turn through this servo. I haven't turned the meter on yet." He seemed to be consoled by this statement.

The service station was not very far away and our position, being on an intersection, it was quite convenient to my task. Heading in the right direction, I turned on the meter.

"What does your nephew look like?" I asked keeping my eyes peeled for a figure walking along the pavement in the same direction as us. Realising that Nigel would be incapable of looking for his nephew.

"I don't know what he was wearing," another reply which didn't help me much.

The road led across the bridge and towards the intersection where I had to turn right. Paddocks of lucerne lined the road leading to the intersection and, thus, not much lighting. It was obvious that I still had been given the responsibility of finding the nephew since my passenger was incapable and incomprehensible. Especially since his body had now slumped into a confused huddle that was incapable of seeking. I strained my sight to hidden pavement.

There was a service station at the intersection that we were now approaching. As the lights were against my turning right I looked into the area around the service station and saw three figures lurking there.

"There are three blokes outside this servo. Would one of those be your nephew?" I asked hopefully.

Nigel, suddenly alerted to my voice as if awakened from a self-centred stupor, replied, "Yeah, that's him." Without, I supposed really looking, due to the positioning of his head.

His sudden and decisive reply made me doubt its authenticity. Although there was lighting around the servo, the figures were still too far away to be certain of the identity.

However I followed the client's directive.

The lights changed and I steered the bus into the servo, slowing as I approached the figures. The figures studied the maxi taxi as well with gazes of curiosity and suspicion.

"Do any of these blokes look like your nephew?" I asked Nigel as we stopped.

Obviously the confusion he had entered into before I asked the previous question had returned. Again he responded abruptly, conscious also that motion had stopped. He tried to sit up quickly, however, due to his slumping and the now entanglement of the seat belt, that proved to be difficult.

Meanwhile the three figures, who had been watching the approach of the maxi taxi, couldn't help their curiosity but investigate why it had stopped.

Two of the young men had their shirts, shoes and other apparel still clinging to their bodies if not totally tidy. The third young man only had his boxers on. He did stand out as being very different, especially considering the night's chill. He was much smaller than the other two but bearing his chest it was obvious that he spent much time in the gym. His muscles showed considerable fitness and his strength was plain to see. He was in the middle of the other two as the taxi stopped but the order was quickly changed as he advanced towards the taxi with apparent evil intent. The other two followed but possibly not with the bare chested one's objective. They seemed more concerned about chasing him.

His eyes glazed with such angry that they appeared to be red. I couldn't understand his instant decision of aggression. The taxi had not been a threat to him, we had only just arrived. Be that as it may, his continued aggressive advance towards the vehicle filled me with paranoia. His two companions caught up to him and tried to stop his advance but they were no match to his violent strength.

Nigel, who had by now untangled himself, especially from the seat belt, and in an effort to see clearly if either of these people were his nephew, opened the door.

Simultaneously the aggro one had arrived and when he saw Nigel accelerated his rage to a higher plain.

"That's not my nephew. This is the bloke who punched me," exclaimed Nigel.

I quickly realised my and our peril. The mad one's fists were now clenched and his voice was reaching a climatic crescendo of anger.

Being more of a passive individual really, I realised I had to fulfil a different role, and quickly.

"Nigel! Can you close the door? Now." I directed which such urgency it even surprised myself.

"He wants to hit me again. Get going, he's on ice," was Nigel's directive to me.

It was obvious that Nigel was going to be of no assistance. In his fear he had fastened his seat belt. This, of course, virtually made it impossible for him to perform the task I had asked.

What was there to do? I couldn't move with the door still open. The punk was set to explode at any moment. I dare not alight and close the door myself for fear of suffering an assault. This would have been rather one sided as I didn't know how to physically fight and thus wouldn't been able to defend myself.

His two companions appeared also to be at their last tether with this maniac. By their attitude it was obvious that they had been trying to pacify this body with little mind for quite some time. However, at this stage of proceedings, they were my only hope. They needed to be motivated.

I searched inside myself to find what little acting skills I had and quickly adopted a persona of competence and authority. Inspired by the impending urgency words flowed through my mouth as though I was chasing an academy award.

"Look fellows, could you get his bloke away from this van, please. I have to get this fella home. I don't want any trouble. I'm just doing my job, all right?"

This display of open honesty and plain talking seemed to do the trick with the two companions. They moved to the task.

"And close the door, could you please?" which they did.

The motor was still running and when the threesomes were clear, I hurriedly drove away.

With heart rate greatly increased by the incident I left the threesome to their plight and I to take Nigel home. Nigel had awoken from his panic and voiced a dialogue about this fellow we had just experienced. Or at least I believe most of his rave was on that topic. His words were most of the time in audible but the anxiety was plain to hear. I hoped that I said "yes", "no" and "fancy that" at the appropriate times.

I made the usual turns to head to his street as he burbled on, but then his voice suddenly became most audible.

"Don't go down this one, there's a better way," he outlined. I followed his directions which were quite definitely articulated. Although I believed this to be a strange way to get to his abode, I followed his instruction.

I thought it unusual that he was now so defined in his navigational abilities until, after I realised we had gone in a complete circle, he pronounced.

"Oh no, I've stuffed up. You better go back the way you were going to go." My faith in my own navigational abilities had been re assured.

The vehicle's motion stopped. To his surprised he discovered he was outside his house. There was a light on inside the house and a body emerged silhouetted against the house. I consoled myself that it couldn't be the puck at the servo and noticed a much relaxed approach to the vehicle, from this figure.

Nigel, realising that his night's trauma was coming to an end, was trying to undo his seat belt.

The body from the house opened the door, and to my surprise, prepared Nigel for the accent to his feet. He appeared to be a gentle young man. He greeted me with gratitude. His care for Nigel was quite noticeable.

Unbeknown to me another body accompanied the man now helping Nigel. This other body was considerably smaller and when it realised the door was opened jumped onto Nigel's lap with great enthusiasm.

The surprise the little dog gave Nigel was not met with suspicion and fear but rather warmth and affection. Nigel now felt wanted and at ease from the night's trauma.

"Ah, little Tiger," said Nigel towards the dog. "It's good to be home."

The man who was assisting Nigel asked, "How much was the fare?"

"Twenty four dollars, forty cents," I replied,

He handed me twenty five dollars.

"Keep the change."

"Isn't he the greatest little dog?" commented Nigel as he caressed the little animal.

"Do you want to give him a pat?" Nigel asked.

I lent over and gave Tiger a little pat as a thank you for loving this Nigel.

Nigel clambered out of the taxi conscious to be careful of Tiger.

As they disappeared towards the house I heard his nephew, Nigel's helper, say, "Thank you."

The Wanderers

It took a while but I was beginning to know the streets. My navigational abilities were improving. Monotony and repetition are great teachers even if it means going around the same circles constantly.

In this learning process it came to my attention of other such similarities. Not just the streets and/or the buildings but the living entities that constantly filled the scenes with constant, cyclical regularities. The living objects could move but was the outcome the same?

A couple, always moving, were an example of this. They would pop up at any place at any time always moving. They looked out of place, as though this was only a temporary existence in this town. This time was to serve a purpose to lead them to the next place where their questions may be answered. No one paid much attention to them. They were seemingly outcasts, living their own path without much interference from others. Not wanting to be a part of any social structure they kept to themselves.

Both appeared to be in their early thirties, although by their very rough appearance and haggard faces, it seemed that they had filled a lot of life's experiences in a very short time. By their sour expressions not all of it had been positive. He was a tallish man and rather thin. His fair hair always seemed to need a styling which was never going to happen. His constantly dirty clothes seemed to be multipurpose, in that they could be used in both warm times and cold. He always took the lead. She followed like a disciple two or three meters behind. He always walked with great pace and I wondered if she had trouble keeping up. She had rather a petite frame. Indeed, if she took the time and attention to herself she could still look quite pretty. It was never going to be while she followed this leader.

Always moving there was never a happy disposition in their progress. It was as though they were being chased or escaping something or they were on an intense mission. By their looks, the vibes they projected, their stern faces always, happiness was never going to be an option.

They filled me with intrigue each time I saw them. What were they doing? Where were they off too? Did they have a home? How did they survive, always moving? What was the journey they were undertaking at this moment? Where was this constant moving, searching, going to eventually lead them? Would they ever be at peace enough to just stay still and enjoy life?

An early Saturday morning, I was sitting quietly in the taxi, in the rank, patiently biding my time, as one does in these situations. Not expecting much activity, it was the Saturday morning lull. They were waiting for the sun to give some urgency to the day.

My innate state was suddenly broken by a loud banging on the passenger's side window. I was surprised and turned to see what this racket was. I saw the face of the male wanderer. He didn't look happy and obviously wanted something from me. I let down the window so he could communicate his need. The girl stood, as usual, three meters away, expressionless.

"You free?" he said abruptly.

"Yes," I replied.

That was their cue. The man opened the back seat door

closest to him and clambered in. The girl, instinctively, went to the other back door.

There were no words spoken as they took their positions.

"Where are we going?" I asked.

"Over to the heights, Cowper street."

I started the car and we moved off. Depending upon the client's attitude sometimes I would try a conversation. It often worked. This was not such a time. Their suspicious gazes scared me off any attempt of communication. A tense silence ensued.

Heading towards the old bridge, nearing a small park at the northern end of the main street, I was given a directive.

"Stop at this park here, on the left."

Not much notice had been given but I managed to accomplish the command. He alighted, gave a careful stare at the surroundings before rushing across to some bushes which bordered the park from the river bank. She sat quietly in the back anxiously looking across towards her companion. He was searching around the bushes for what I did not know but it seemed to be very important.

His arm reached into the forage and pulled out a plastic carry bag with something in it. He didn't hesitate in his return. She appeared more relaxed upon the find. He looked carefully upon the scene before entering the taxi again.

When he was secured and without a spoken word, I set off on the journey again. Across the bridge and I wondered if my curiosity about this couple was going to be satisfied.

It was not. The walls around this couple were well defined and impenetrable. The journey was spent in silence.

I entered Cowper Street and was told the house in which to stop at. The house was not your well to do affair. It was the type of house I would expect these to come to. It looked very uncared for and given the number of children's toys scattered about the yard, it was logical to assume it was not their home.

Seat belts unlocked, they seemed ready to confront their mission on this Saturday morning. I was given a cash note as the fare and he waited for the change.

The change given, he headed off with his expressionless face. She chanced a slight smile at me in appreciation. I worried after her.

No words spoken, he led the way to the front door of the house and she followed religiously behind.

The Weirdo

If it was my aim to meet a host of different people in this vocation I was not being disappointed. Although, it was my lot to be on the outside looking in. It had become apparent to me that this seemingly inauspicious small country town had a great diversity of inhabitants. Some of them had definite aims and others with no direction at all. They did have a common thread in that they were all just going around and around in the circle of life's experiences.

One of the twin hotels in the centre of town had rooms for lodgers. When the hotel was built it would've been very popular with squatters who faced a long and arduous journey home by horse and sulky. These days, with a host of motels on the highway, they were filled with people who had nowhere else to live. The rooms were not of a five star standard and really left a lot to be desired. Yet they were always full.

The rooms were upstairs towards the back of the hotel. The lodgers would prefer to be picked up by the taxis at the rear of the building.

Isaac had become a regular customer. He was a young man, in his early twenties, tall and thin with an already receding hairline. His hair was deep black. The very long length at the back, often tied up, seemed in compensation to the thinning amount of hair behind his forehead. He was never fashionably dressed, in fact I never saw him out of dark blue track suit bottoms. The garments covering his chest did have variety depending upon the temperature. His tee shirts in summer were usually brightly coloured. Or at least they were before too many stains revealed the duration since a last washing. In colder times the dark pullovers hide the grime. I had learned to keep a window down a bit even in colder times to let in fresh air as it was evident his personal cleaning shared the same time lapse as his clothes.

He did not fit into any criteria. A true bohemian with which I could relate to. He was more concerned about today rather than next year.

His most accentuated trait was his extreme hyper energy, bordering on manic. Always restless, always buzzing, always stressed to perform his mundane tasks for this day.

I first encountered him not long after I had started. The rank was not very far from the back of this hotel. Parking in this place was easy and I waited for the client to appear. I spied a figure leaning over the verandah upstairs. He seemed to recognise that this was the lift he had ordered. Upon realisation his movements were swift. He literally bounced down the staircase and I assumed his journey was in haste. In preparation and sensed acknowledgement that this was the client, I had the car started in readiness.

His manic energy and distinct aroma was evident as soon as he clambered aboard.

"Where are we off to?"

The dialogue that followed was said with such pace and urgency that I found hard to take on board.

"There's a wreckers up on top of that hill out of town a bit. Do you know the place?"

Fortunately I did know where he was referring to as they were the only wreckers in town. It was just as well as he didn't wait for my reply.

"They reckon they've got a starter motor that'll fit my car. That's my car there...."

I observed a small Toyota parked with dust laying over it.

"It stuffed up on me coming into this town on my way to Queensland. That was weeks ago and I've been stuck here ever since. It's not easy on the dole trying to save enough to get it fixed. This pub's all right though. The publican knows my story. Then there's the trouble of not being ripped off. Got to be careful, you know, getting these parts. They'll take you if they can."

The journey to the wreckers took us over the bridge. Whether he was aware of our progress was debatable. He seemed more interested in talking, nonstop, not waiting for a reply. It was as though he talked for the sake of it. Obviously he didn't do it very often and this was his chance to exercise his vocal tones.

"I know me mate's waiting for me up in Queensland. I should've been up there a month ago. He wants a hand with some stuff he wants to do on his land. I can't ring him to let him know what's happened and I don't have one of them computer things, but he'll know why I'm not there."

I couldn't help but ask "How?"

"I think on him. I lay on my bed up there and just concentrate on him and conveyed what I'm up to by that. It's all in there you know man, it's all in another dimension. All the thoughts are there in that space. All we need to do is link into that place. Then send him the message that way. I know he's into that stuff so I know it'll get through to him. It's not as we can see it, it doesn't have any physicality, its just thoughts. It's like before you do anything you have to think of it. Once you've done that you can then do the physical things that have to be done to make it work. You know what I mean?"

He didn't wait for my reply but assumed that I did.

"Everything you would want to know is there man. It's the total of all knowledge. It's in a world that most of them don't even know about. Some of them call it God. But it hasn't got any personality, it is just thoughts. No point praying to it, the future is already written, it can't be changed, chance will win in the end and we have no power over that. There is no grand design and happy endings. Fate will take its toll and all the plans change, so why plan? All we can do is have good thoughts and then you'll attract other good thoughts. If you have bad thoughts you'll be on a downer. It is all a matter of attitude. If you want to have a good time you'll have a good time no matter the circumstances. It is just your attitude that counts."

Unbeknown to Isaac, we had arrived at our destination. He realised it when the car had stopped. Gone was the philosophical rave on religion and all things spiritual as reality kicked in. He paid in cash and headed off without another word. He was on a mission. I presumed that he didn't want me to wait for him as no words along that design was pronounced.

Months had passed and as chance would have it I received a call to Isaac. As I drove to the back of the hotel I wondered on Isaac's current circumstances.

He was downstairs by the time I had gotten there. He was standing near to his car with the usual stressed nee manic expression on his face. I noticed that his car had collected more dust and I wondered upon its fate. In anticipation I had the window down a bit even though this day was a little cooler.

It was a wise decision his aroma hit me as soon as he clambered into the car. Not of a personal smell but rather, I suspected, emulating from his clothes which showed a considerable conglomeration of different stains.

"Where are we off to?"

"I think I've gotten my hands on an old push bike. We've got to go out of town a bit though."

He gave me the address and I then knew where I was heading to.

"You picked me up once before didn't you?"

He recognised me.

"What's your name?"

"Scott. What's happened to your car?"

"It won't go."

"The starter motor didn't work?"

"No, they ripped me off, the bastards."

He sat in silence for a bit as I navigated my way onto the country road leading to the destination. It troubled me as he was so talkative on the previous fare. I wondered if he had gone into a meditative trance to the other side. The other dimension he had talked about during his the last journey with me. I was wrong.

"It's all a conspiracy, you know. It's an evil that is creeping into the other side. It's infesting the place. There's too much of everyone wanting stuff for themselves. Only for themselves and never for anyone else. You can't blame them though it's what they are led to do. They are trapped into doing what they are told to do....."

I couldn't help myself but break into the rave. "Who does this?" I was surprised that he registered my question.

"The capitalists. They are the bastards. They rule everything and make everyone fit into their designs for greater profits and bigger egos. Look at all these people, running around consuming stuff they probably don't even need but they are told that they do so they go out and buy them. They've all gone crazy, running around doing what they are told to do so the capitalist can make a profit. They're cunning, you know, the bastards. They tell them that they will be happy once they buy their stuff. And what gets me is that they believe them. How dumb is that! Then they tell them they need the next gimmick to make them happy. And so it goes on and on. It's stuffing the place up, you know. The capitalists can't exist without growth and profits. But the world is a finite space, what's going to happen when there is no more room for growth? The whole place will implode. Not enough food to feed the masses and then see their profits crumble. Then they'll wonder why. They are so dumb. It's disturbing the other side. It's lost to them all as they wonder around the shopping centres. There's no hope if peace can't be attained. How can they find a peace in themselves if they are always wanting for something?"

I knew that I must've been approaching the desired destination. It was confirmed when I saw a driveway with the obligatory mailbox with a number on it. I slowed down. Isaac's lecture came to an end.

"You don't have to drive up to the place. It should be next to the mailbox me mate said."

I couldn't see anything like a bike until.

"There it is, laying on the ground there. Wind must've blown it over. I hope it works all right."

I pulled into the drive way and stopped. Isaac paid his fare in cash. I wondered if there was some purpose for this bike being where it was. My query was answered when Isaac lifted up the bike and I could see the word "FFreebie" written on a piece of weathered cardboard, hanging from the frame.

I too was a little concerned that the bike was operational. I waited whilst he check it all out.

"It's a little beauty," and I felt relieved.

I left him to his journey back to town on his newly acquired push bike.

Occasionally I would pass him, on his push bike, as I traversed the town with my driving tasks. His long hair would be flowing behind the obvious second hand helmet. He always seemed on a mission as he pushed hard on the pedals. Maybe he was trying to beat chance and take control of his life. I kept noting, though, each time I went past the back of the hotel, how his car had collected more dust.

One day I spied him on a skate board entering the shopping centre where I was parked in the rank. I also noted people desperately getting out of his way. His mania was obvious, again. He did see me seated quietly in the taxi. He recognised me. He stopped next to the window on the driver's side so I wound down the window. I figured he was into a chat.

"I remember you. You took me out to collect that bike."

I didn't have a chance to reply before he latest rave started.

"Those greedy capitalist have taken over the government. I figured it all out. They use the government's propaganda to keep us all consuming. That's what it is all about. Work to spend. Keep them in little circles of work and spending such as change is never a threat. It keeps the rich richer and all them dickheads out there trapped into what they are told. And they believe them, that's what I can't understand. Don't they know what's going on? It's all a conspiracy, you know, they are all out there to control us absolutely. I'm all right though. I've seen through them. I can go to that other place, the other side, where their silly little ego games fail into insignificance. I'm only dictated to by chance and none of us have any power over that. Things just happen that we have no control over. Not even the capitalists."

At this moment, as chance would have it, the noise went off in the taxi indicating a fare. He heard the noise and it alerted him to my reality. He tweaked it.

"You have to go?"

"I'm afraid so mate."

"See you next time."

With a sudden push in his skateboard he was gone.

I didn't see him for a number of weeks. Then as I was passing the back of the hotel I chanced to notice that his car was no longer there. Instead I did see his bike, with no chain on it and the now very crumpled sign of "Freebie" decked across the handlebars. Questions unanswered but I liked to think that "chance" had maybe dealt him a good turn and he was on his way to the other side at his mate's place in Queensland.

Sam

Some people are happy, some people are sad. Their situations are irrelevant compared to the attitude they have regarding their lot.

Saturday afternoon was the shopping afternoon for Sam and her family. She was very regular like the procedure had been inbuilt into her program for many years.

There was always a smile on Sam's face when she would present herself at the taxi rank with piles of shopping bags. Never booked for the return trip as she knew she could save a few cents by chancing a vacant taxi.

On this day I was the first in line and thus I received the friendly. "Are you available?"

In her mid thirties, her attire was very casual as though she had no care for what people thought of her. Her self confidence could ward off any negativity. Her dark brown straight hair was always tied back. For practical reasons I thought. A big framed lady but not overweight, she carried herself with an infectious energy that was always positive.

Today she had her oldest son, Josh, with her. He never said too much but always adhered to his mother's requests. He also had a big frame for his early teenage years, but different to her in that he took after his father, Jake, a pacific islands man.

I would meet Jake when we would arrive at their address. He would be waiting at the front door. When the taxi pulled into the driveway he was ready to help with the groceries.

His face would never show much expression. Rather a stern predominance. However behind the hardened demur one could sense the existence of a very fair, righteous and considerate man. He was a good bloke.

The love shared between Sam and Jake was plainly evident. It flowed easily onto their children. I felt great joy to see them.

As usual there were two full trolley loads of full plastic baskets to fit into the sedan. She had a big family to feed. I opened the boot and Josh was ready to fill it up. Sam supervised the operation, instructing Josh where to place what. In the meantime she was filling the back seat. The operation went very smoothly. Originally I used to try and help but realised they always had it well under control.

They lived in a small fibro cottage in the south end of town. It wasn't very elaborate but they kept it tidy, as opposed to the house on their left.

There were no walls around Sam. What you saw was what you got. Her conversation was always genuine and abundant. Often one didn't even have to press the start/conversation button before she'd break into full voice. On this day, as a follow on to the previous chat, I took the lead.

"So how's the bloke next door treating you?"

"Oh him. He's gone a bit quiet lately."

"Did the police come around?"

"Eventually. They didn't find anything. I reckon he must have a pretty good hiding place if you ask me. Still get the loud music at ridiculous hours of the night. I still reckon he must be on something to be like the way he is. Now he looks at us with even more hate. I just wonder what his problem is. I tell the kids to keep right away from him. We caught him wandering around our place one morning, looking for something. Jake reckons if he sees him again doing that he'll wish he would never have come near our place. It's not fair on Jake either he's got to do shift work. I wish he'd move. He's got problems. He hardly gets any visitors. The ones he gets don't want to be seen. They sneak in and out. Wouldn't have a clue if he has parents or not. He seems too young not to have some sort of connections. He always looks at everyone with such hate and yet none of us have anything to do with him. He's just a case and I wish he'd move"

I'd always considered Sam and her family were a little out of place in this street in the unfashionable part of the town.

"Or you could move?" I asked slyly.

"Don't want to move, it's the kids home for the moment. Besides its cheap rent and we're saving a bit of money It might not be flash and it sure is not what I had in mind when I was in my early twenties. Back then I was saving money like crazy, doing whatever job I could get where I lived in Sydney, just so I could jump on a big jet plane and see the world. I wanted to be free and do and go where ever I wanted to, Was good though I learnt a lot of skills doing different types of jobs. Comes in really handy when you're travelling you know."

"So did you get to travel?"

"Oh yeah. I worked my way up to Darwin, working in different outback pubs. In Darwin I scored a really good job as a receptionist for a big travel mob up there. Made me some really good connections there and it got me a free ticket to Bali."

"What was Bali like?"

"That's where I met Jake. Back then we were going to travel the world. Get jobs where we could. Jake's a boilermaker so he can always get work and I didn't mind what I did."

"What happened?"

"I got pregnant. We had to find a home and job quickly. We came here and have been here ever since. Jake managed to score a good job in the mines. Stuck in this house till all the kids get to go to school. Then I could then get a job and get us out of this street. I could put Jessie into preschool now, but I rather have them at home. That's what I've done with the other two. I'm their mother and this is their home, not some stranger in some unwelcoming building. That's what has made us such a close family."

"One day perhaps, you'll be able to head north of Bali again."

"I can't see that happening for a while. The kids'll have to be left school, and we'll probably have a mortgage to pay off. We will just become like everyone else trapped into the cycle of bills and pay checks. I'm not complaining though we really love our kids, they are better than somewhere over the horizon any time."

The Mansions

I often admired the wonderful rich alluvial flats that surrounded this town. The white settlers also fancied this district. They had discovered agricultural haven within fifty years of the white settlement. After that the first nation people had to move. Such was the way of the European invasion.

As expected they did very well but not without the toil and hardship to make it that way. So there it lay for decades, a quaint little town on the banks of a flourishing river, servicing the properties. The decedents of the pioneers reaped the rewards of their predecessor's hardships.

A culture or social structure soon evolved. Not dissimilar to that of the British Feudal system of the middle ages, the property owning barons and the peasants that served them. The natives were outcast to fend for themselves. Certain church service times were only meant for certain people.

It was a week day, just after school finished. A busy time with many of the taxi drivers involved with taking children home. I was left holding the fort, stationary in the rank. I knew it would not be long before I'd be in motion again.

Sure enough to an address I was not familiar with. Upon investigation and with the navigational aids on hand I realised this was out of town, heading towards the army camp. Being an "out of towner" and realising the other drivers would be busy, I felt a certain need for haste in my progress.

I turned right onto the road leading to the camp. The bonnet of the taxi began to point a little upwards as the vehicle began to ascend a hill. I knew there was a turn off to the left. I peered for an indication.

It came. Sandstone walls acted as sentinels to a ramp. By the dullness of the stone it was obvious that they had been subjected to decades of the harshness of this environment. The eroded soil on either side of the ramp also gave testimony to the wear on this entrance.

The trail before me, lead through an open paddock. To my left was a picturesque and elevated view of the railway line, the highway and also the glorious river flats beyond. The view generated by the hill had been half climbed. To my right I could see cattle grazing on the higher slope. I wondered if they marvelled at the view as well. The track was dirt and corrugated in parts. It was a further indication of age. I could easily image how this was once traversed by horse and buggy.

The track headed towards a ridge with a fence line making it. A slight bend and I could see the path leading to another ramp through the fence. Given that this ramp was on a ridge line and having learned from the previous ramp experience, I approached the ramp with extreme caution. My calculations proved correct. No damage to the vehicle, just a bit rough for the driver.

Upon realising this test had been passed I could turn my attention to the next obstacle. The trail continued down the ridge towards my destination. I was stunned at the sight.

The two seemingly out of place Victorian mansions that caught my eye as I entered this town all those months ago had always fascinated me. There was a tale within those walls that I was curious to discover. I was about to find out.

The most outstanding feature was the two towers that marked the edge of the building at its front. They gave notice to the first floor. Although the design was obviously based upon Victorian architecture the palatial verandahs at the front on both floors with their stone pillars and wide windows show an appreciation to the environment. It was a variation upon the theme of English standards.

As the building came further into view I could see the walls were made of large sandstone bricks, similar to those at the entrance. Also similar to those at the entrance they were showing of their age. The bright yellow at their instigation had now faded to a dull and inconsistent creamy colour. A dull, almost brownish, red covered certain features like window shades and certain beams. The different colour to the sandstone would've given it a rather distinguished look when first built.

Two very tall pine trees stood as guards to the building facing the view. By their age they oozed enticing tales. Despite its obvious wear the mansion still held a certain charismatic presence, a relic of the times now past.

As I drew closer to the building I could see a late middle aged woman seated on a very stylish breakfast setting, shaded by the verandah, near the front door. She realised her lift was arriving even before I could see her. She was collecting herself, making sure she had her hand bag and her keys, before making herself more visible to the driver. The driveway itself was a circular one which obviously led to the front door. A welcoming and grandeur sight for any visitor to this residence.

As I approached her eye contact made certain my purpose in this venture. She walked with dignity belying her encroaching years. She had pride in herself and she was on display, status on show.

Being a rural lady she was not dressed as I would've expected. Not the akubra hat, tightly fitted. Not the colourful, button up at the front shirt, not the tight fitting jeans and the always polished riding boots. But a creamy dress which came down to her ankles. She wore a beautiful navy blue coat and a stylish pair of shoes. Maybe it was a little old fashioned, but certainly distinguished in appearance. A little above everyone else as if to say, "this is the way to do it". Her stateliness befitted the residence.

Such was her presence and appearance I felt compelled to alight from my driver's seat and hurriedly make my way around to the left hand back door, to open it up for her. She saw me coming and waited for me to fulfil my task.

"Nice to see there are still gentlemen in the world," she said as she climbed into the back seat.

Directions given, I placed the vehicle into drive and steered my path around the circle and onto the open paddock entrance road I felt a distinct status difference. I was a mere taxi driver and she who was in her finery. However, being polite, I chanced a conversation starter.

"It's a very beautiful house, you must be very proud of it?"

She paused for a moment, possibly not expecting a taxi driver to start a conversation. (They should know their place). However, perhaps it was that because of my courtesy she concluded this man had some breeding and thus worthy of a reply.

"Yes I am. I just wish I could fix the place up a bit though."

"Still looks pretty good."

"Not like it was when my great, great grandfather had it built. It was the envy of the valley then. People were honoured to be invited. They used to have balls in the main hall, once, countless afternoon teas, dinner parties. Oh yes, this was the centre of society in those days. I still put on afternoon teas, you know. Not many of the old crowd left now. The district has changed. The coal miners you see, they aren't our type."

"So who built the other mansion?"

"His brother had it built, just to prove himself in front of his sibling. They never got on, you know. Their father owned all of this land right down to the river. He was one of the first to settle in this district."

"That's a lot of country."

"Oh yes, prime river flats. He did very well but did it tough. When he passed on the boys took it on but they could never agree, so they split the place. Hence the mansions. These two buildings were the pinnacle of their success but they were also the downfall. The expense in having them built and then followed droughts, then floods. All the gains got swept down the river."

I took it steady crossing the grid at the entrance. We were now on a main road. In me she had discovered an attentive ear. She continued.

"Of course, over the years with each climatic disaster more land got sold off. I've still kept the homestead and this country on the slope. I rent some of it out to fellows who want to place their cattle and keep the home paddock to myself. At least I've kept it in the family name. The other side went broke. They had to sell that mansion as it was the only bit of land that they had left. That was about twenty years ago. Some lawyer fellow from Sydney bought it. He had big designs to turn the place into luxury hotel. Nothing been done since and the old place is falling into rack and ruin."

I turned onto the highway, heading towards the town.

"And all these people here now, all these cars, they wouldn't even be bothered to know about what's gone on before them."

"So what will happen to the estates?"

"I don't know. I've got no one to leave it too. They should be made into museums, displaying the years of the pioneers to this district."

We passed the speed limit sign, I was slowing down.

"This is the place here on the left. I just hope they have fixed the car up properly this time."

I manoeuvred the taxi into the yard of the biggest and most prestigious car dealership in town. Her dialogue now stopped as there were other things on her mind. She passed me a fifty dollar note and waited for the correct change.

"Thank you young man," she stated sincerely as she alighted from the taxi. Steadying herself and gaining the composure befitting her stature, she was ready to deal with her task.

A spritely young man must've seen her arrive and with a broad smile greeted her. His approach seemed to have been planned as he would've been told that this lady was part of the landed gentry of the district. I figured that her car was ready and the taxi driver was no longer needed. I left her to fulfil her role as part of the aristocracy of the district.

Stuck

I wondered about the woman from the mansion. She represented a history, not only in a pioneering sense, but more specifically in lifestyle. Cultural structures that were set and maintained, all knew their place. That was the way it was until coal was found in the district. A subtle new regime then invaded the area. These new enforced immigrants had no respect for previous social structures. There was more money and more jobs from coal production. The squatters were now on the back foot.

More jobs needed more homes. New residential dwelling were established on the other side of the river. The bridges had to be crossed to reach them. These dwelling were much more modern and functional. They represented the new influx of wealth into the area.

Saturday night and the meter had been working steadily all evening. Now it was time to take them all home from their night's outing in the town.

The pickup point often indicated the type of client. A call came to a recently renovated pub turned into a stylish restaurant. It was designed to attract a better type of clientele.

The usual place to park was not the most convenient. One always hoped that the wait for the client would not be long. At this time of night that hope was often forlorn as, after a few beverages, the taxi driver was of least consideration.

I waited. Texts were sent, but still I waited. Eventually a

couple emerged and noticed the taxi. A sure sign these were the clients. They were in their early thirties. Both appeared to be rather "well to do", as though they filled important positions in the community with well paid jobs. Another couple of comparable age followed them outside. They swayed a bit, unsteady on their feet after a long session of sitting and consuming, as their prolonged and over emphasised farewells continued. It was night's end for their social interaction, and the happy smiles and louder than necessary voices conveyed as much.

They appeared to be both confident in their movements as though they were used to being "a little better than everyone else". Both were smartly dressed, or at least by this town's standards. He wore a collared shirt without a tie and newly bought jeans. Her flimsy pink dress swayed lethargically from the soft easterly passing through. The dress moved in a different direction once the finality of the evening had arrived and the taxi was now the focus.

The doors open abruptly as though there was a certain urgency to the effort.

"Lot 4 Cassidy close, do you know where that is?" asked the man.

I knew that area. It was situated over the bridge beyond the new section. It was well away from the more suburban streets and the cluttered house blocks. This area had acreage and was designed to be exclusive.

"Yeah," I answered at which point there seemed to have been placed a wall between the back seat, where they both were, and the front seat, where I was. Their conversation needed no involvement from the driver.

"But how can they afford it, Brad?" she said.

"He got a big bonus last year, Lee. His mine out there is

going gang busters."

"So where is this place they are talking about?"

"Out along the Brestone road. It's not as glamorous as they are saying. It's a subdivision of an old grazing property, split up into one hundred acre lots."

"They were saying that it was an old established property which had been in the same name for generations."

"They may have said that but the truth is there are for sale signs on it stating, sub division."

"What about having a cattle stud there?"

"On a hundred acres! You know what they are like. It was just another pose."

"Pose or no pose, they are doing it. And we'll only be on our five acre place. What about the house they say they are going to build, it'll be a mansion. Just a little cottage, she says."

"Yeah I know."

"I'd hate to know how much they are now in debt."

"They must reckon they can afford it all."

"They are getting around us, that's what they are doing. They'll have more than us then. What are we going to do about it?"

"Save up and get a bigger place than they've got. A real farm. We'll be one over them then."

"On what we earn? It'll take years. What about that promotion you're going to get? Any word on that?"

"Still in the pipeline."

"It's been there for months now."

"Once we get the cars paid off, and the boat, we'll be in a better position."

"I don't know why we got that boat, we hardly ever use it."

"They got one, remember."

"That's right."

"What about your hair dressing shop? Can we make more money out of that?"

"It wouldn't be a tax dodge then. Besides ever miner's wife is doing it now. The word's out about that scheme. There's not enough hair in this town that needs to be cut for all of us."

"Perhaps we could put off going to Bali this year, or even stay at a less expensive hotel?"

"Oh no, if we're going to go, we go in style. Imagine if they found out we stay at some dump. Five star or not at all. Besides, we have to go now. We've told them that we are."

"We might have to put off doing those improvements to the house then."

"You need to do something about that driveway. You can't see the drop in the dark. Someone's going to do damage there at some stage."

"That needs doing."

"We'll have to put off having kids for a bit longer then."

Their discussion continued past the street lights and now into the darkened and exclusivity of the privileged sect. They were completely oblivious to the ears listening silently in the front seat.

As I turned into their little enclave the insular verbal exchange in the back seat suddenly included the machine with feelings, the driver of the vehicle.

"The second place there on the left."

I was pleased for the inclusion as the exact driveway was a little hidden in the night. It was surrounded by thick bushes of Grevilleas. Being on the side of a hill the driveway pointed up through other well established flora. Eventually an expansive roof of what was a very large house began to reveal itself.

Now that the barrier had been broken with the taxi driver, silence, as we progressed up the driveway prevailed.

The driveway pointed towards the garages with the house to the right. There was a small area of available parking in front of the house.

I headed towards the garages thinking I could reverse into the parking area when leaving.

The vehicle placed into park mode, journey's end for the clients. A card appeared through the darkness of the back seat as payment, without the prompt from the taxi driver. The amount seemed to be irrelevant.

Transaction completed the back doors opened and they alighted. The doors banging was the punctuation mark to end the interchange.

Remembering the parking area behind me, I reversed carefully towards it. The area was still in darkness and I had to trust the memory of my glance at this space.

The vehicle turned slowly with the house on my right and absolute darkness on my left. Suddenly with a crash, I felt the vehicle tilt markedly towards the back left. I was going nowhere.

"What have I done?" I thought with panic.

Gears into park and engine turned off, I alighted to see what had happened. In the darkness I could now see that on the edge of this small parking area was a retaining wall and the drop below it. There was nothing to warn of such an obstacle, like some vegetation or a barrier, just a drop. The passenger's side back wheel was now hanging precariously over the edge. I was going nowhere. I needed help of some description.

The lights were now turned on in the house. Terribly

embarrassed, I knew I would have to approach my ex clients. I knocked on the door and waited. The wait seemed endless as I was uncertain how I would be accepted or even if they would or could help.

The door opened as though the opener was suspicious as to what to expect. When he realised it was the taxi driver he was more relaxed.

"I'm sorry mate," I began, "I've got the car stuck over the retaining wall."

"Who is it?" Lee's voice sounded from within.

"The taxi driver." And then to me, "Come on then let's see what we can do."

He led the way towards the garage and with a press of a button the doors of the complex opened. Complex it was, it housed an early model Porsche, a boat and at the end a latest model four wheel drive. It was towards this vehicle that Brad moved to.

Lee appeared from the house as if something was happening and she wanted to be a part of the action.

"What's going on?"

"Go and get that good torch will ya?"

Brad started up the four wheel drive and started backing out. I was surprised that he didn't first inspect what I'd done. He had the vehicle reversed in front of the taxi when Lee appeared with the torch. It was then that the inspection took place.

"I keep telling you that we should put something up here. You're not the first one this has happened to." Lee said.

"I said I'm going to do it."

"Yeah, when?"

Without a word and with a seemingly little bit of annoyance, which I think emulated from Lee's remark, Brad fetched a tow rope from the back of his vehicle. When I realised what he had in mind I helped the connection to the taxi.

Lee kept the light to the relevant places as if by routine. Brad and I assumed our positions in our respective vehicles and without much bother the mission was accomplished.

I was free to depart. I thanked them both profusely as I still felt as little embarrassed that I had to trouble them. They impressed upon me that it was no bother at all.

Our interaction now had an unexpected appendix which turned out to be a helpful and pleasant interchange.

Chris, part 4

In our journey through this passage called life, one is going to come into contact with others of our species. It is virtually unavoidable. What's more, especially being a taxi driver, one has little control upon who one is going to come into contact with. It is all a matter of chance.

Often from the first impression, you instantly know that you're either going to like this person, dislike this person or see this person as just another client. With a positive vibe shared it would usually lead to a pleasant and enjoyable conversation. If the vibes were negative the silence was often only broken by the report of the final fare. Of course this first impression, the initial meeting of vibes, does not interfere with the professional approach one has towards the passenger. They don't need to know what you really think of them. Conversely they are not too concerned about the relationship with the taxi driver. At journeys end the relationship also ends, maybe never to be re kindled. Fleeting glimpses into another's soul only to end abruptly. Was I looking for a soul mate where the journey didn't end?

I was not going to meet that person in a taxi. I was not going to find that person in my tiny little abode. After a day of interacting with people, when I got home I was always grateful to spend time with myself, alone. My relationship with my workmates, although pleasant during a shift, ended at knock off time. It was only I who knew my true self. Others only saw what I wanted or needed them to see. Was this what I wanted? Is this how it is in this realm of a human experience of partial connections? It had virtually been like this all my life. But then isn't this the game they all play? Displaying only that section of oneself that best suits the situation, for practical reasons, and the real self is only for oneself. Was I looking for someone that I could dissolve my walls to?

The miles increased during my journey as a taxi driver in this town, without really going anywhere. There was one exception though. This particular journey was taking me on a very beautiful drive through very pleasant countryside.

My passenger on this journey through this scenery of fantasy always shared with me such wonderful vibes that I would look forward to the next encounter. It appeared that this feeling was being reciprocated.

As it happened, there was more bureaucracy to be conducted and more time with Chris, in her office. Although underscored by the fact that time was always of the essence, at procedures end perchance time for a normal conversation. Nothing very profound, simple day to day topics, not dissimilar to conversation pieces experienced in a taxi excepting that this fare, through the positivity of the connection, was not going to end. There was a mutual joy in our relationship.

I didn't know if I properly understood. We still hardly knew each other, least of all her to me. What were her circumstances? Why was she so seemingly interested in a taxi driver at least ten years younger than her? There were still unanswered questions that I was keen to have answered.

Late autumn and the weather was rapidly changing to a bitter cold. A heavy storm passed through in the night before my day off. The morning presented itself as a day to stay inside and keep warm. The news was reporting damage and road closures.

I was set for a day indoors, watching predictable faces on a screen. The phone rang, which was very unusual. I didn't get many phone calls as, since I never stay in one place for very long, I didn't have many friends. I dreaded that it might've been the boss wanting me to cover for a shift on this very cold day.

It wasn't the boss. To my great surprise it was Chris.

"I'm sorry to disturb you on your day off but ..'

At this point I assumed that it was something to do with work. I felt the dread of having to leave this warm abode.

"That storm that went through last night has knocked down a big tree branch on our place here. I know it's your day off but I'm wondering if you could come out and help me clear it all up, please?"

Suddenly the dread of going outside in the cold faded into insignificance. Affirmation confirmed, directions conveyed, I was setting out on a different type of journey. Were questions going to be answered?

In reality I still didn't know a real lot about Chris. I wondered why it was that she rang me for assistance. She had lived in the district for much longer than I surely she would've built up her own network of friends, etc that she could call upon before me.

The directions led me along a road that I had not yet traversed. It was all new country and I enjoyed the escape. I did notice, as I got closer to the address how much debris from the gum trees had fallen onto the road.

It was good to be out of the town and to enjoy the countryside. Little abodes on smaller acreages nestled in the tranquillity of open space. Keeping a close eye for numerals on mailboxes I slowed to find the right address. I turned left to follow a dirt path down to a small brick house. As I drew closer to the buildings I could see that great care had been taken to maintain a beautiful garden. The Camellias were in full bloom and they gave hope to a dismal looking day.

The house was a sixties design. In its day it would've been quite modern but time had loosened its appeal. The garden was now the highlight. As I approached the building I was uncertain as to where to find Chris. The house was the obvious place but as I looked further beyond the house I could see other buildings and some horse fences around one of them. I then spied a figure of what was obviously Chris jumping vigorously trying to attract my attention. I headed the prompt and headed down to where she was.

She was near a stable. I could see a horse's head peering out of the shelter. I could also see where a branch from a gum tree had fallen over a perimeter fence, breaking some railings. For the time being the horse was staying inside. Quite a job lay before us.

The biting wind caught me as I alighted from my car but her welcoming smile quickly returned the warmth. This was a different Chris to what I had known at the office. Chainsaw in hand, tools collected logically, rope handy, she presented as one who knew what was to happen.

She was obviously pleased to see me arrive. Her task looked overwhelming and the extra hand was going to help.

She handled the chainsaw with obvious experience and I carried the logs and placed them in a neat pile. We paused for a bit as she re fuelled and sharpened the blades.

"Timber cuts well when it's still green."

"You look like you've been on a farm for some time. Were you born to it?" I asked.

"Oh no, I used to work in an office in Sydney when I was younger."

"What prompted the move here?" I asked innocently.

My question met with an immediate negative reaction. I worried that I had said something wrong and I wanted to backtrack. But what could have been wrong with such a simple question?

Her immediate negativity was forcibly being rectified to suit the present company. I could tell that she was changing tact so as not to reveal something that was to remain hidden.

"Things changed." She said solemnly.

I didn't enquire more. Soon after the chainsaw sparked into life and we were once again into it.

The miserable day was changing despite the weather which stayed constant. I felt very warm, either that I was doing a physicality or rather that I was enjoying being with Chris. I felt a real connect between us and almost wanting for the work not to end.

The branch was transformed into convenient proportions in a safe place. Railings sourced and placed with precision. The horse was watching every movement that we made and now that he could see the railings fixed started to become restless. Chris' attention was now drawn to the animal. I stood back as she went to the stable door.

"Have you ever had much to do with horses?"

"Not much."

"Come over and introduce yourself to Zac."

The camaraderie between the two was obvious. I could only but feel secure. I did know to hold out my hand as I approached the horse to let the horse smell it. The horse appreciated the gesture and we both felt at ease.

"You see, you did know something about horses."

She moved inside the stable and beckoned me in as well so as to shut the stable door. The horse stood calmly as she started to take off his horse rugs.

"My darling has been stuck inside here all day and it's time to get out and play. I won't be able to work him today, I haven't enough time, they'll be wanting me up in the house soon."

As the rugs came off it revealed a very athletic individual. I chanced a guess.

"Thoroughbred?"

"Ex racehorse. Didn't like having his feet going along the ground all the time, he just likes to jump where his feet can fly. Don't you?"

Rugs off and safety assured, Chris opened the stable door and Zac bolted out into the yard. The magnificent athleticism of his body was well on display as he frolicked about his yard.

"They like to be free and not penned up in a stable all day."

Admiration concluded as practicality took place. Chris disappeared for a moment to return with a fork and wheelbarrow. It was mucking out time. I helped and she talked about her plans for Zac, the three day event was her go.

"There's an event coming up in a few weeks time, I hope I can go to it."

Her love for her horse was profound. He was obviously a centre of her life.

"I wouldn't have anything if I didn't have Zac."

Stable maintenance completed, sinus cleared by the ammonia, day work seemed to be coming to a conclusion.

"I would like to pay you for your help. I couldn't have done it without you."

I insisted that payment was not necessary amongst friends. I could feel the urge from both of us to now have an open chat. At last the chance to reveal ourselves.

However the enthusiasm was suddenly broken by her phone. She answered it and instantly I could tell the positivity of the previous conversation was quickly diminished. Her expression changed to one of convention and daily routine.

"I'm sorry but I have to go. They need me up in the house. I'd ask you in for tea but they're not very well at the moment."

I could see the urgency in her and realised this interaction was coming to an abrupt end.

As I drove away I felt sympathy for her. She obviously would've preferred to be with Zac and myself but her commitments, whatever they were, prevented this from happening. I wondered about the tie that enclosed her.

Happy Ending

Autumn was making its presence felt. Not just jumpers but coats were now being found to accommodate the change of season. I was spending a quiet Saturday afternoon, mainly sitting in the taxi, inside the shopping centre. I was safe from the depressing outside scene of low clouds and not much sunlight. It was only to get worse as winter approached.

A call came through to break the chilled stupor. Not unusual at this time on a Saturday. The train would've just arrived from Sydney and someone would've wanted to get home.

Into gear and soon I was approaching the railway station. It looked dark, gloomy and lonely in the fading afternoon light. I noted a single person staring at my progress. It didn't take much effort of my cognitive processors to realise this figure was my client.

I pulled up beside the woman. I could see her relief as I did. She had a number of bags, some of them closed and others open with garments hanging out of them. The coat that she adorned, had all the marking of being recently attired, feeling the chill of the outside air. Wrong buttons in the wrong button holes was the evidence. Maybe that was an explanation for the untidiness of the open bags.

She was an Asian woman with a gleaming cheerful smile that seemed to challenge the day's gloom. I alighted to place her luggage into the boot. Her exact age was a little difficult to ascertain as she wore a considerable amount of make up to seemingly hide the reality. In her youth she would've been quite petite and attractive, but a certain amount of middle aged spread belied the past. But the energy she transmitted also belied the middle aged spread. She seemed determined to stay young and her demeanour showed it.

"Hello," I said as I approached the luggage, wanting to start up some form of communication.

"Hello darling," she responded.

She watched which items I attended to and then proceeded to pick up the rest. Together we placed them into the boot. We were close enough for our bodies to come into contact. Upon finishing the task I noticed that she placed her hand softly on my shoulder and then ran it slowly down my arm.

"You're a nice boy for doing that, thank you baby."

I was a bit taken back by this sudden and unexpected show of flirtation. It was not normal, especially since we had hardly even met. But I placed it down to a cultural thing or perhaps that was just the way she was. Our journey now needed placement into the vehicle. I to my usual position and the lady could choose. She chose the front seat. She told me the destination by leaning across the gap between us such that the scent of her perfume was prevalent.

Wishing for a more normal conversation I asked, "Been to Sydney?"

"Yes baby, I had to get some sexier lingerie, what I've got is getting worn out. They don't have those sort of shops here in this town."

Upon saying this I noticed that she was observing me very carefully. I could feel the full beam of her eyes upon me. Keeping to a professional approach though I tried not to notice. Even when she moved her hands to rearrange her breasts under her garments, I kept my eyes on the road.

"Do you like it here in this town?"

"It good work here. They have army base here. Plenty of young boys wanting my services. They have plenty tired muscles. I make them feel better. It good money here."

Our destination was not very far away from the railway station. She also realised it was not very far and that the encounter with this driver would end soon. She was in a hurry to make her intentions clear.

"Even coal miners need their tired muscles seen to."

She placed her hand onto my lap and started rubbing her hand towards my groin.

"Maybe even taxi drivers too, baby?"

This move did make me feel a little uneasy.

Knowing I was on the street where she needed to go and in an effort to distract her from her current motivations I asked, "Your house is somewhere along here?"

"Near the end of the street darling."

The distraction didn't entirely work as her hand stayed on my lap, threatening to move.

"You very handsome, baby. How come we never met before this?"

"Perhaps you never needed a taxi when I was on call before." Was the best response that I could muster under the circumstances.

"We should get to know each other better baby. I like you."

This response left me completely lost as to what to say in response. It would be a lie to reciprocate her feelings towards me.

Fortunately the end of the street loomed and I could uncover a plan of escape.

"Somewhere here is it?" As I search for house numbers.

"The white house on the right."

Journey's end, I could escape the hand on my lap with definite purpose.

The white house, as she described, although being on the south side of the highway, was quite well kept and looked inauspicious. It was as though it was just a normal house. But the sign in bright red and blue flashing lights registering "Open" belied its normality.

I helped her with her luggage as far as the gate. I wished to go no further.

She was very grateful to the extent where she chanced a little peck of her lips upon my cheek.

"You should come and see me sometime. I make you feel really good. You so handsome I give you discount."

Before I could give a reply I could hear the noise from the taxi signifying another fare waiting. It gave me a response.

"I have to go. Good luck."

Aunty Rose

Saturday morning in autumn, the COVID restrictions were becoming more acute, again. Although, to many of them in this town, it still seemed to be a headline which only affected other places. They were doing their shopping despite the current restrictions, so involved in their chores, time was of a premium. All were in a hurry without much heed of the precautions now in place.

A call came from an address that I was now familiar with. The destination did however give rise to some concern. To the railway station at the neighbouring town about forty minutes drive away. The concern was that often the passenger would not allow enough time to get to a railway station. This drive, being of a distance, the chances of delays were also greater. Trains don't wait.

The house I was going to was occupied by Aunty Rose, an elder of the local indigenous community. It was never a straight forward drive with Aunty Rose. Variations often interrupted predestined routes.

I arrived at the address. Sometimes she, or someone living at her address, would notice the taxi arrive and I wouldn't have to wait long. Sometimes this didn't happen. I hoped that on this occasion, since there was a deadline, that I would be noticed.

The house and block were always easily recognisable, even without looking for the number on the letter box. It always had the longest lawn, it always had articles laying across the lawn.

Implements, toys, iron objects, it was interesting to note the procession of articles on display. This day was no exception excepting that there was a lawn mower standing idly in the middle of the lawn, seemingly waiting to be engaged.

At least a couple of minutes had passed since I pulled up in the driveway. It was that time when one began to consider the next course of action in order to have been noticed. Especially since, on this journey, there was a deadline.

She appeared through the door with her head still focused on the inside, calling.

"Hurry up Colin, the taxis here and I'm in a hurry. Lock the door when you come."

She sported a walking stick on this day. Some days she would appear with a walker. Those were the days when her tired hips were playing up and the walker was necessary. Not this day, she progressed down the path to the taxi with a renewed sense of enthusiasm and dignity, befitting her role as a community elder.

Dressed a little bit better than what she usually wore. Her hair had been washed and tidied. The dress was clean. It gave her a certain charisma that I hadn't seen in her previously.

"And bring my bag out with you when you come. Hurry up. I've got a train to catch."

She looked at the vehicle and I saw her shoulders sink in relief. The maxi taxi van that I was in this day would be easier for her to get into. I could tell by the way she progressed slowly down the path that this was a difficult day for her limbs although she was trying not to show it. I alighted to open the door for her.

"Come on Colin." She yelled with indignity.

Colin appeared through the door, closing it tightly as he

came. He was not attired nearly as neatly as Aunty Rose. His filthy jeans appeared as they had had limited exposure to the washing machine. His T shirt had some inscription on it but due to the grim on it, it was unrecognisable. Apparel for the feet was not an option. He was tall and thin, he struggled with the load of Aunty Rose's suitcase. His foot placing seemed confused as if he didn't know where to place them with the load, engaged. I wondered if this was a representation of his mind.

He hurried down the path to reach the door as Aunty Rose was contemplating the step into the van.

"Put the bag in before I get in."

The directive hit Colin with confusion and I considered that my initial thoughts upon his mental capacity was, indeed, correct.

It was proven by the fact that he placed the bag in a place that was going to interfere with her accent into the maxi taxi.

"Don't put it there. How am I going to get into the bloody thing with that in the road?"

He realised his folly and moved the object to a more practical space.

After much concentration and determination, whether it was real or put on, Aunty Rose managed to place herself into the vehicle. Colin followed like a secondary subject in a royal procession.

As I assumed my seat the variation upon the destination became apparent.

"We gotta take Colin to them flats at the end of Menzies street, you know the ones, you've been there before. Colin did you get that bit of paperwork off the table, I left it there for you?"

"I forgot," was his feeble reply.

"You better go and get in then. Hang on mate," she directed me before I had placed the vehicle into gear. She fumbled through her bag which showed similar age to her and eventually found what she was looking for, the keys. She handed them to Colin.

"Here you are and hurry up, I'm in a hurry."

Colin left for the purpose. His feet seemed to find greater accuracy now that he wasn't loaded with a weighty burden.

As he disappeared from earshot Aunty Rose commented.

"He'd lose his head if it wasn't screwed on properly, that one."

A momentary pause or silence ensued as the impatience of the wait reigned. I had learnt that Aunty Rose did like to chat. It was only a matter of pressing the right buttons or in this case saying the right words.

"So where are we off to?" I asked.

"Sydney."

"What's on?"

"We've got a big demo on tomorrow. I have to go, I'm representing our mob up here aren't I? They'll probably get me to talk again."

"Will you be able to get to Sydney? I mean they've got all sorts of restrictions on travelling now."

"They can't refuse me. I'm an elder, I've got important stuff to do."

A hurried Colin re appeared from within the house, documentation in hand. As he moved towards the van Aunty Rose called out with a voice that the neighbouring block would've heard.

"And lock the bloody door."

Colin reversed to the door as I also prepared to reverse out of the driveway. He entered the van in a hurry, handing the keys back to Aunty Rose. I waited until he was safely placed before setting the vehicle in motion worried that the sudden movement might set his limbs out of balance.

"Now you've gotta take that down to that office where we were the other day. It's been signed so you shouldn't have any problem. You got that?"

"Yeah." Colin replied.

"You gunna do it tomorrow? You won't get anything unless you do."

"Yeah all right."

The van in motion, impatience filled the air. There was a distance to go with no idea of any more variations. I turned into the street directed to me.

"Now tell James to come and see me when I get back."

"But he's skint now."

"I haven't got time to see him now. By the time you go and get him out of bed and decent enough to see me, I can be half way there. He'll just have to see me when I get back. He should've come with me yesterday when I was down the streets."

I arrived at the address. A set of flats with what used to be uniformly attired had now become individualised through untidiness. The van came to a halt.

"Hurry up, get out of here, I've got a train to catch and you've holding this bloke up."

Colin alighted with haste. Door slammed shut, I wondered what the next variation might be.

"To the train station?" I asked with hope.

"Yeah, and you better hurry up. It leaves in three quarters of an hour." I was relieved to hear this.

Just as I was about to set the task into motion, I noticed a half clad man in his thirties come rushing out of the complex. He seemed in a hurry if not very anxious. It was obvious that the maxi taxi was his purpose. He passed Colin on the footpath without acknowledging him although it was obvious that they were acquainted.

"Oh no, I didn't need this," remarked Aunty Rose who now had realised who this person was.

The body reached the maxi taxi and forcibly opened the door.

"Where are you goon?" His voice expressed with urgency.

"I told you James, I've got to go to Sydney for the big demo tomorrow."

"But you said you were going to give me some cash to tide me over."

"Yeah, that's what I said. I also said that you'd have to come down the street with me yesterday so I could get the cash out of the bank. What happened to you?"

"Yeah well I forgot."

"Well that's no good to me then is it?"

Meanwhile the engine was running and I was trying not to be noticed as I chanced a glance at the time. I was conscious of the train's departure.

"Haven't you got any cash on you now?"

"No, I bloody well haven't. I'm not going to go on a train and go to Sydney with a lot of money on me. You never know what might happen to you, especially down there. You'll just have to wait till I get back now."

"But I'm skint."

"Can't be helped. You didn't make it yesterday so you'll just have to go hungry. That might improve your memory. Now fuck off, this bloke's got to get me to the railway station and we are wasting time."

Dejectedly James closed the door in defeat.

The pressure was now on. There were two ways to get to this neighbouring town that has an express train to Sydney. The conventional route would see us going through a series of villages, each with their own traffic complications that can only be time consuming. The other way was longer but used the new free way and thus no hesitations. The latter was always my preferred option, especially when time was an issue. I kept my plans to myself hoping that Aunty Rose would have confidence in my navigational abilities and experience.

Manipulating my path through the streets of houses onto the highway, she was not so much focused on my route.

"They're bloody well unreal, aren't they?"

I ascertained she had something to express.

"Last week I had no one coming to see me, no one ringing me. Then I get my compo cheque through and I'm suddenly the most popular one in the world. Should've kept me mouth shut, that's what I shoulda done. Bloody Colin's got to pay a fine or else they reckon they'll lock him away. So I've got to help him out. Bloody James' frig has broken down, wants me to buy him a new one. Bloody hell, I'm not made of money. Then there's second cousin's daughter wants to move away from that rat of a boyfriend of hers and needs money to get herself moved. What can I do, I've got to help them out too. At this rate it'll be all gone and nothing for me self."

The worry of getting red lights as we headed out of town proved to be correct. We got them all. I kept an eye on the time.

The correct buttons had been pressed and Aunty Rose chattered gleefully as we headed out of the town. I learnt about her sister and her siblings. The rotten bloke she got as a husband. How the eldest can't get a job, although Aunty Rose reckoned he wasn't trying very hard.

The rhythm of her rambling suddenly changed, however, when she realised we were not going the way she would've thought we would go.

"Hey mate, aren't we going the wrong way?"

It wasn't as if I wasn't expecting this reaction. Although the new freeway had been in operation for over a year, some people, the ones that don't go out of their patch, weren't familiar with its path.

"It's quicker this way."

"But you're going the wrong way, it's over that way, I bloody well don't want to be late for the train, you know," she stated pointing to the direction.

"You wait and see, it'll head in the right direction in a bit," I tried to say as reassuringly as I could. By the mood emulating from the back and the momentary silence I concluded that my reassurance was not successful.

"Yeah well I hope you know what you're doing. I don't want to be late, you know."

In another attempt to be reassuring I tried another tact.

"So what's going on with this demo tomorrow?"

"It's gonna be really big. There'll be mobs coming from all over the place."

"What will you be doing?"

"They'll be getting me to talk at the big gathering at Hyde Park. I'm important, you see, I represent the local mob here, you know."

I had pressed the right buttons and she seemed much more relaxed whilst having something to talk about. Until the unfamiliar scenes which the freeway presented had awaken her to new stimuli which now controlled the conversation.

"Gee, I didn't know any of this land existed. It's all right this new road, isn't it. You can get along a bit on it can't ya."

Unfortunately, by the time she had realised all of this, I started to decelerate to turn off the freeway towards the per destined town. This had not gone unnoticed.

"Where are we going now?"

"This is the way to the railway station. We're heading in the right direction, now."

I seemed to get the impression, by the vibe from the back, that there was a considerable amount of hope going on, as she wasn't now familiar with the local surroundings.

"You better not be late."

The set of red lights uncounted and the abundance of traffic added to her concern. However, as we topped a rise and the view of the railway station became obvious, she felt relieved.

"There it is, gee that's not a bad way to go, is it?"

As I pulled up outside the station I notice we had arrived ten minutes before the train was to depart. To Aunty Rose, however, it seemed that the train was already on the platform waiting for her. Her excitement was growing as she realised that her fantasies about this trip were now coming to a reality. She hurried out of the van. The walking stick now assumed the role of a prop, bag in hand with no great difficulty, she prepared to ascend the stair onto the platform. I wished her good tidings.

"Yeah this will be a couple of days that I don't have to worry so much about our mob back home, I'm not there. But I will be when I get back and it will all start over again. They'll be all wanting something from me."

The Bag

Winter was heralded by a day of constant rain. Not heavy but enough to make the day miserable. All seemed very quiet excepting the constant beat of rain drops. It was a subduing tempo which kept all indoors and taxi drivers in their vehicles. It was a day where one ends up watching the clock.

A call came, which broke the monotony, an address in the southern part of town. Off on a mission. The windscreen wipers created another tempo which added a further stimulus to this day. Any other intrigue was welcomed.

The address revealed a house which was probably once cared for. However the "not for years pruned roses" gave a more current story. I waited with now only the rhythm of the raindrops as entertainment.

The front door opened and exposed a head and shoulders but no body. The eyes saw me and seemed to tentatively exit the house. He was middle aged, wearing an old pair of jeans topped by a dark blue sloppy Joe. A large black beanie covered his head and much of his face. It was obvious he didn't pay much attention to the way that he looked, his half shaven face was further proof.

He was followed, in turn, by a younger man, perhaps in his mid twenties. He looked anxious and followed some distance behind. He too sported a large black beanie which, apparently, served the same purpose. A large coat covered his body such that it was difficult to ascertain his body shape. This was further complicated by the fact that his left arm was holding something under the coat. He held onto this object very tightly.

The leading man had reached the rusted old gate. He paused before opening it. The gate made a noise revealing its age which was instantly frowned upon by the man. In order to stop this racket he lifted it up a bit which bought about the stealth he was after.

He didn't protrude onto the street with any confidence. In fact, as with when the front door of the house opened, his head appeared first in a moving pattern which took in the view of all parts of the street. I wondered why he would do this, given that it was such a miserable day, the chances of a collision with another was highly unlikely.

Satisfied that danger was not an option, with a brief glance he looked back at the younger man. He had been standing still, half way down the path, while the older man's head peered onto the street. As if on cue they both moved with a certain precise choreography.

The older man opened the back door closest to the house as if to enter but didn't, rather left the door open and proceeded to the other back door. By the time he had opened the other back door the younger man had arrived and again, with precision, both entered the car simultaneously. As was now expected, both doors closed together so as to only make one sound. As per planned, a quiet sound.

As they began to settle I noticed that neither had their face masks on. It appeared to be one detail in this process of gaining access to the taxi that they had over looked. It was a necessary action that I had to undertake on this particular week, but was disappointed that I had to break with their carefully laid out plans.

"Sorry fellows, you'll have to put your masks on."

'Shit, that's right. How could I forget that?" the older one said.

He paused a moment to ponder a change of detail.

"Quick, go and get a couple of masks. They're on the table in the kitchen, you'll see them. Leave the bag here."

The younger man now revealed what it was he had hidden under his coat. It was a small carry bag. Made of dark plastic, it had no disguising features excepting that it was currently a prized possession. Whatever its contents were it filled a greater proportion of the bag.

The younger man left for the purpose. I could sense a certain "we're behind schedule" vibe emulating from the older man.

In an effort to speed this operation up I asked,

"Where are we off to?"

His answer was given rather gruffly as though his mind didn't want to be disturbed from its present subject, or that he didn't want to reveal too much.

"I'll show you the way. We've got a few places to go to. The first one's over the railway bridge, heading south."

An impatient silence filled the taxi, excepting of the rhythmical beat of the raindrops.

The older man looked anxiously towards the door and I could feel a distinct relief assume him as the younger man re appeared. His now more relaxed state seemed to prompt him to make some polite conversation to the taxi driver to demonstrate his social graces and place the taxi driver at ease, thus not question any of the pair's purpose.

"Been busy?" he asked.

"No not really. The rain and this COVID stuff keep's everyone inside."

The younger man re united with us and they placed their

face masks on.

"Do a Uie and head towards the railway bridge, there."

As though, as a taxi driver, I didn't know how to get to this bridge. However, due to his self appointed, superior status I figured it was his way of taking control of the journey.

A tense silence again ensued, broken by the raindrops and now to add a variation, the windscreen wipers.

"They'll be there?" asked the younger man.

No audible reply came from the older man however I did catch his finger placed in front of his lips which said more than sound. In an effort to distract from their purpose in the eyes of this taxi driver, to ensure that I held no suspicions, the older man again started a conversation.

"Bloody nuisance this COVID shit, isn't it mate?

"I guess we just have to get used to it."

"I think it's all a lot of crap. It's just another way the bloody government is taking control. As for getting this jab bit they can go and get stuffed. I'm not doing it and no one's going to make me do it. It's all rigged you see, someone out there is going to push a button one day and all these silly pricks that have taken this jab will be under the total control of the regime. That's what they want you see, total control of everyone. Fill them full of paranoia and bullshit about dying from this man-made virus so as they all flock to get the jab and then they are all stuffed. They are real bastards they are."

His conspiratorial rave continued after we had crossed the bridge. The road then headed out of town. I wondered if a country drive was imminent.

However the tone of his conversation suddenly changed.

"You gotta turn left up here."

I slowed for the process.

"Then left again."

The steering wheel was active.

"Now down here there's a blue house with an old wreck outside it."

"I see it."

I slowed down and parked opposite the appointed domain. Restlessness became apparent in the back seat with a bit of anxiety thrown in.

"Just wait here will ya mate. You can leave the meter running, we won't be long."

They alighted with again precision. The bag was firmly in the clutches of the younger man. They were men on a mission. They disappeared into the house and I turned off the engine and listened to raindrops. The raindrops continued for quite some time. Occasionally the beat would intensify to then die down to a steady beat. Such was the current stimulation whilst waiting.

The meter had now chalked up more than the actual drive to this house before I noticed the re appearance of my clients. They hurried towards the car, carefully observing a street with no one on it. I started up the car as they climbed aboard.

It was noticeable that there was a certain vibe of satisfaction as though the mission had been successful.

"Right oh mate. We've got to go to the other side of the highway. Go up the main street and under the overpass and I'll show you from there."

The main street was usually a slow process but on this day, due to the restrictions and the weather, we progressed quickly. Silence emulated from the back seat. Their mission was still in their thoughts.

The underpass divided the town. Once transverse the shire offices loomed with the Catholic Church in the background.

However the church was not to be passed.

"You've gotta turn right up here mate."

Instruction obeyed.

"Then into this street on the left."

Unsure just how far up this street I was to go I progressed slowly alert for further instructions.

"This white house on the left."

I did well to travel slowly, it was short notice.

"Leave the meter going we won't be long."

Bag in hand they entered the house. Again it was only the raindrops to fill me with inspiration. Waiting, waiting, the mind becomes very bored. At least the meter was going, a real "trading your hours for a handful of dimes" situation. Along the street, my only visual entertainment realised that nobody came and nobody went on this very uninspiring day.

My mind had entered a very stationary mode when something different did, in fact, happen. A car entered my vision through the rear vision mirror. Minuscule as it was it filled my cognitive processes during its progress up this street. Only to be interrupted by the front door of the white house opening. It was all happening. My clients also viewed the car. They stopped and watched the car travel slowly past with a suspicious glaze. Once the car had passed and it was obvious that it was not going to stop, they moved quickly, again with precision, back to the taxi.

They, like after leaving the previous house, seemed quite satisfied.

"Right oh mate, we've got to get to the other side of the highway."

"Up here, turn right. When I get to the highway, which way from there?"

"I'll tell you when we get there."

He hadn't told me much. Added to which, with all the through traffic on the highway, going to other places, in a rush to get out of this town, it was going to be difficult to turn right. I waited anxiously as we approached the intersection. My destiny was in this man's commands.

"You've got to turn right up here,"

This was the worst result. I hoped that, since it wasn't much of a day, there wouldn't be that much traffic. Not so, cars and trucks advancing from both directions. Weather doesn't stop the tyranny of distance. The only hope was that traffic lights at either end of this thoroughfare would simultaneously unite to give a clear passage. It needed patience. I tried to be cool under this pressure and wait for the correct opportunity.

I could see a break in the unbroken parallels of moving vehicles but it needed precision, timing and courage. I felt confident that this tactic could work. The gap loomed and I accelerated quickly to be soon travelling west with no interference to other drivers. Done, and I was pleased that there were no police around to see what I had just done. The feeling that I got from the back seat seemed to also be relieved that there were no police around.

After an anxiety release the older man spoke, and not before time.

"Turn left at this next street."

This directive bought about a massive change in driving practices as the order was given very late. It meant that I had to brake hard and turn instantaneously. Not good driving and certainly conspicuous, however it was successful.

"This green house on the right."

In keeping with the other destinations, this house wore the

same characteristics of neglect.

"Leave the meter running, we won't be long," came the now familiar words.

Bag in hand and carefully watching the surrounds the two men crossed the road with haste.

Again a solace of perpetual raindrops commenced, however so boring. At least this street had more traffic passing through it which gave me something to be mesmerised by.

The minutes ticked by. The raindrop rhythm became now tediously boring but still I had to wait. The only consoling fact was that the meter still ticked. Boring as this current waiting was, it was possibly better than at a taxi stand earning nothing. This was the third waiting session and I wondered how many more there would be. They re emerged and the answer was imminent. They entered as I started up the car again. Again that vibe of satisfaction was apparent if not greater this time.

"Where to now, mate?"

"Back home."

I started moving off without instruction. I knew the way and, as their mission was now completed, his need for authority was no longer needed.

"You know the way then?" he asked.

"Sort of'" I said dryly.

"How long you been driving taxis for?" he asked trying to appear as though he really cared for me, or perhaps it was to say to me that they were really nice guys and that I shouldn't wonder upon this expedition they had just led me through.

"Nearly a year in this town." I replied.

"You probably know your way around this town by now then."

"A bit."

There appeared to be now no more paranoia as they disembarked. In fact there seemed to be a joyous satisfaction. The plastic bag was considerable empty. The fare was considerable but the older man had no hesitation is paying it plus a fifty dollar tip in cash.

As I drove away I recounted my words. "Nearly a year in this town." The words occurred in my thoughts as a razor blade through a thin wall. The cut opened up an underlying thought that I had been neglecting. What am I doing here? What am I discovering in this place that will aid me in my quest for the mountain of wisdom? Am I to look at the walls in my little abode and wonder "what if?" Am I going to descend into little tight circles within the sixty kilometre zone? Like all these people who express themselves upon me in quest of an answer? Am I just the taxi driver who can produce a mirror to their sole and remain just an object without life, thoughts and feelings?

Stan

The vibrancy of the summer had passed. It was now winter, with its sombre, almost depressing chill that dominated the atmosphere. The day had started with a dense fog which seemed to prolong the night. It was not till 10am that headlights could be turned off. The passengers hurried from their houses across to the vehicle of conveyance so as not to feel the bite of the cold that was now permanent.

The fog had lifted but by not very much. Into the afternoon and the sun was still not visible. All waited with patience and hope for its appearance. Not to be till the late afternoon when the night was already heralding its presence of a greater cold, did the feeble sun poke through.

It was the type of day that the end of the shift came as a great relief. The weather on this day was not conducive to pleasant thoughts. The only hope was home as a sanctuary of fantasy against the over bearing cold that was quickly forming the role dictated to by the night.

Logging off duties done, I ensured that I was appropriately rugged in anticipation of having to transverse the passage of cold from the taxi to my car. The night driver, beginning his shift, approached the vehicle as I alighted. His face bore no expression which conveyed a certain mood of solemnness. He knew the night was only going to get colder and he was not looking forward to it. A few brief words exchanged only to be polite as the warmth of our destined vehicles promised more comfort than the outside air where the conversation was being conducted.

I was hoping that what warmth there had been during the day would've persisted in the car. Upon placing my body inside I was sadly disappointed. Hurriedly I turned on the ignition and immediately the heater, waiting impatiently for it to combat the cold.

Any semblance of sunlight had now disappeared and it was realised that the headlights functioned quicker than the heater. The sanctuary of a home and comfort away from this uninspiring day now beckoned.

As humble as this little flat was, and as cold as it now appeared to be as I entered, it gave a certain warmth of domesticity and sanctuary. I again reverted to a prism of isolation and time to oneself, peace at last.

A shower promised the quickest way to attain warmth. Once done, now time to settle into a free time at home. Suddenly the phone rang, as if a reminder that there was a world outside these walls. It jumped me from my solitude and forced me back into reality again.

"Hello," I answered, in a surprised voice as if this was unexpected.

The voice that followed was immediately recognisable.

"Scott, I know you've probably knocked off but I'm short of night drivers tonight, a couple of them haven't turned up."

I sensed, from my employer's voice, that my night was going to be disturbed and the cold engaged again.

"There's a truckie broken down about 150 km up the highway. Apparently he's at that truckie parking bay just after you cross the river. He's waiting on a spare part. I can't send any of the blokes on tonight as that will leave me short here.

Could you take it up to him, please?"

His tone was as nicely, as politely as he could possibly make it, but with a certain "you will do this for me" attitude. It was as though I was always going to be compelled to do this task because he was the boss and had asked appropriately. At least I was allowed to take my car with a flat rate guaranteed.

Flat locked and whatever warmth had accumulated during my stay would now quickly disappear. Into the absolute cold of the car, it was now after 7 pm and firstly I had to go to a spare parts place to pick up the part.

Upon my arrival I could see, by the expression on the face of the proprietor, that although I might've caused him a chilly wait, he was pleased to see me. His duty done, for him home beckoned. The package to be delivered didn't take up much room. It was a small cardboard box with a secret ingredient that would create a much needed salvation to the receiver.

With this small box as my companion, we set off towards the darkened highway beyond the concluding street lights. The darkness of a country road did not appear very welcoming. Occasionally it was broken by the harshness of the oncoming headlights, impatiently piercing into the passing cars as though they were a hindrance to the path to their warm homely destinations. It was the type of night where no one wanted to be out in.

Certainly not I. The further the journey progressed the less was the traffic till seeing another car became a novelty. The darkness prevailed on either side of the car, only the headlights gave any indication beyond the black. I thought of the truckie waiting for this part and that was my companion. How long had he been waiting? Was he by himself? How cold was it for him stuck in the middle of nowhere on a cold night?

These thoughts tended to depress my accelerator pedal.

Besides the sooner I got there and delivered, the sooner I would get going home.

My new found enthusiasm was dealt a blow by the fact that as I was travelling on river flat country, and the fact that the air was quite still, fog was beginning to descend. Not wanting to slow down too much I kept my eyes well concentrated and on high alert for any wandering animals that may stray onto the road.

The fog was thicker as I approached what was to be my destination. It hid possibly landmarks that would've telegraphed my position. All I had to go on was the fact that I had to cross the river and that bridge would be my landmark. Where was it?

Already on edge with the constant peering for animals, I now had to be prepared for ......   And just as suddenly as I was anticipating, the bridge loomed forbiddingly through the fog. There were no oncoming headlights and I concentrated on preparing to transgress the structure. Its wooden flooring seemed to crackle under the weight of my vehicle as if ice had already formed on it.

I knew the destined parking bay wasn't very far from the bridge. Through the fog I peered to see the turnoff. I was hoping that the recipient may have his lights on and that would be a sign. The blanket of mist revealed no such illumination.

At last and quite suddenly I spied the break of guide posts on the left and the tell tale tracks leading to the parking bay. I knew this was the place. But as I turned my vehicle left the darkness invaded. There was nothing to say this was the space. Certainly there were no greeting lights to herald my arrival.

Eventually as the vehicle turned towards the central position of the bay, the truck came into vision. It stood destitute against the forbidding situation it found itself in. The darkness and lifelessness of the scene gave the situation for the truck a certain existential feel.

I could make out the load. The shape of which was unmistakable. Huge tyres reached up past the mist into the darkness. The type of tyres used in coal mines. The truck by its size had the capability of carrying such a load. It dwarfed my little utility. I parked and turned off the lights. At that moment the full extent of the blackness of the night portrayed itself with ultimate prominence.

The place seemed lifeless. Where was the driver? Why weren't there any visible signs of urgency and distressed? I knew there was a small village about two kilometres away and I wondered if the driver had walked into the town for a drink to pass the time.

I waited in the total dark for some minutes. Perhaps I was disappointed that after my determined dash across the darkened landscape that I was not being instantly gratified. What to do? Outside the car promised unbearable cold but sitting doing nothing wasn't going to get me home any quicker.

It was time to investigate. I opened the door of the car and the cold rushed in. This impact created a desire to get this operation over and done with as quickly as possible so as to the experience the car's warmth on the return journey.

Through the complete darkness and the swirling mist I could still make out the outline of the truck parked opposite. As I approached the stationary combination of metal objects that seemed like a permanent sculpture I hoped for some sign of life, to give the structure meaning.

I paused hoping my approached may have stirred some life into the situation. Obviously not, the stage remained silent. I stood next to the door of the cabin. However I had to look up at quite an acute angle to see the door's entrance. Worth a knock perhaps, that might spark life into this object that had been persisting through the increasing cold.

I clenched my fist and reached it up into the mist to target the door of the truck. Loud enough so as to stir any life in the structure but soft enough as to not disturb the peace the night, the cold and the mist had created.

The silence continued for what seemed a long pregnant pause, and I wondered. Suddenly a light appeared from within the cabin. I was relieved but at the same time curious as to what was going to eventuate.

The light shone feebly out of the cabin and didn't seem to dent to soberness of this night. A shadow then emerged peering outwardly as to inhibit the power of the weak light. The shape the shadow created obviously resembled a human, but the definitions still remained a mystery. As long as the figure stared into the void of the night the greater was my curiosity.

Perhaps this figure, silhouetted against the cabin light, was wondering where the noise had come from. Certainly his long gaze suggested as much. But surely, even though the light was weak, he could see me. I moved hoping to gain some recognition. It bought about an immediate effect.

Eventually the door of the cabin opened and the figure began the first signs of movement. Although the cold of the night must've been quite a shock to the figure now presenting itself, there was no sign of a reaction to it. This body, now revealing itself, was merely clad in a tight singlet and shorts. The singlet was so tight on the body that I could sense the outline of an extruding waist line that wobbled when it hit the ground.

His stare was now aimed directly at my, shivering from the cold, body. The feeble light from the cabin now illustrated, partly, one side of his body. I could see that the grey hairs on his chest protruded out of the top of his singlet. His pale blue shorts had stains that appeared to be permanent fixtures. Stretched woollen socks fell over the laces of his once brown but now blacked boots.

Although I sympathised with his situation his greeting and a very smiling face showed no sign of stress. The over welcoming, friendly vibes he was sending me made me feel instantly relaxed in the company of this stranger, met somewhere in the middle of a darkened nowhere.

His voice perfectly represented the character I had quickly sensed.

"You got that part for me, have ya?" He asked with a certain knowing, but with a little uncertainty, hope.

His smile intensified when I replied in the affirmative.

"It's in the car."

I ventured across to my vehicle for the purpose.

"What's the time?"

"A bit after nine," I replied.

"I must've dropped off to sleep."

"How long you been here?"

"Must've been about half past two or there abouts. I knew what was wrong with it as soon as it happened. I thought about bringing a spare one when I was leaving but reckoned it'd get me back home. I didn't."

He accepted the parcel with glee and proceeded to undo the wrapping.

"Why they put all this crap on it I don't know. It's only a small thing anyway. Could've just given it to you and I wouldn't have to go through all this"

"Where's home?"

"Toowoomba in Queensland."

"You're a long way from home?"

"Just helping a mate out, you know. He was a bit short due to this COVID bizo."

"How far you got to go?"

"Only a couple of hours to the mine from here. Nearly made it."

I watched him clamber back into the cabin. His late middle aged body struggled a bit but with determination he made it.

"Don't like getting in and out much these days. Hurts me knees too much."

I watched him fiddle around in the scarce light. Suddenly, without warning and totally unexpectedly, the whole area was radically transformed.

A series of very bright lights filled the entire parking area with such a violent impact as to scare off the peace that had reigned.

I was taken back but he wasn't. Excitedly he again struggled out of the cabin but only as far as to fiddle around with the metal enclosing the engine. It was immediately apparent that his tried body had performed these tasks before. I thought of possibly asking him if he wanted a hand. His body moved with such confidence through the procedure that I figured that I would only have been a hindrance. Besides my shivering body was now feeling the effect of the cold. The lights had not dispersed the temperature.

"Bloody pleased you made it here so quick, mate. I thought I might've been here till any old time really. At this rate I'll, depending how long it takes them to unload, I'll be heading back before dawn."

"You going to get some sleep before you head back?"

"See how it goes. I've just had a few hours then."

His body was now half submerged into the engine. He had arranged the lights such that he could see what he was doing.

There was really not much for me to do now that my task had been completed. The thought of the warmth in my car began to emerge but my curiosity about this fellow kept me shivering.

"You've been driving trucks for a while then?" I asked even though the answer was obvious.

"Yeah I've done a few trips in my time. I reckoned to myself the other day that there's not many roads in Australia that I haven't crossed at some stage or other."

"You must like it then?"

"Yeah, I like being in country. You might be in a small cabin but it seems to give me great freedom of space. Makes you feel a part of it all, you know. Great country for driving in this place, you know. Beautiful it is. Missus, up in Toowoomba, doesn't mind. She says it get me away for her. I wouldn't tell her this but I don't mind being away from her either."

Paperwork signed, his engine running it was time for us both to be left this place and return it to tranquillity. I wondered if he would remember this night as a part of the many journeys and difficulties he had travelled. It seemed that to him no obstacle was too insurmountable to be passed. It was merely run of the mill stuff. His journey through the wide spaces would continue and his peace complete.

Warm again, alone again, driving on the way home. Through the darkened landscapes without the urgency of before, I pondered Stan, the truckie, his acceptance of whatever fate was going the throw at him, his resilience to deal with it, his contented demur. The peace he had found in himself. being constantly apart of country and the good will that transmitted.

Paul, part 3

July and the days had become very short. What limited sunlight that did occur after the fog had lifted provided a false fantasy of potential warmth. The mood was gloomy, faced with the prospect of this chill to be continued for months to come.

Parked in the taxi rank at the shopping centre hoping for a fare so as I could start the engine and thus the heater.

In a bored malaise trying to convince myself that it really wasn't that cold, I caught the image of familiarity exiting from the centre. And a most unexpected figure when I realised who it was. Seemingly out of place to our usual routine.

Paul, accompanied by a shopping trolley, which seemed also out of place, eagerly looked upon the taxi rank with hopeful intent. Relieved he saw that I was waiting in the cold and apparently ready for his need. Our eyes met and without a word being spoken I reached to find the lever to open the boot.

I alighted to help him with his unusually big load of shopping in the trolley.

"Having a party?" I commented upon his large load of groceries.

"That would be right."

I helped him unload his purchases of items in little plastic bags. He pushed the trolley over to a safe place and we assumed our positions in the taxi.

"Stocking up for winter, is it?" I asked rather tongue in

cheek, awaiting a humorous, in character, reply.

"Well I've run out of food, haven't I. I hate coming to these places, too many people, but I had to."

"And they are all so badly behaved."

"Riff raff."

"So how come you've had to do the groceries?"

"I haven't seen the bloke she organised to do it all for weeks. Don't know what's happened to him."

"Where's your wife?"

"Over in London again."

"You didn't want to go with her?"

"It's a cold miserable place, what would I want to go there for?"

"Might be warmer there than what it is here at the moment."

"You been to London?"

"Yes."

"What was the weather like?"

"Miserable."

"See."

"But that was in April."

"Doesn't matter. It's miserable all the time. The wife reckons summer happened between three fifteen and four twenty last Saturday. Then it started to snow."

The car's interior warmed up as did the exaggerated truth, but it was all entertaining. I didn't broach the topic of Carlton's disappointing season until.

"Bloody Collingwood keep winning. I hate Collingwood."

"I think St Kilda plays them soon."

"Come on St Kilda, beat the bastards will ya?"

The amusing interchange was coming to an end as his house loomed. Cash exchanged with a little tip.

"See what you can do to beat Collingwood, eh."

"I'll give you a hand with the groceries, if you like?"

"Would you?"

To me it was a chance to get another laugh out of him, a help in trying to brighten up this very unappealing day.

The change in temperature caught us both and we hurriedly collected the plastic bags. He led the way and paused while he found his keys to unlock the front door.

The door opened and I hoped it would be a bit warmer in the house. It wasn't.

"Bloody cold this place in winter. Now you know why I'm always in the back room. It's warmer in there."

We passed through a hallway adorned with beautiful old furniture and ornate objects d'art. It oozed old world charm befitting of my friend Paul. Also to be noted was just how clean and tidy the interior of this house remained.

Although there was not much light in this hallway, almost as though it was permanently kept this way, at the end of it, however, I could see a small light from the ceiling that appeared to be permanently on. It shone onto a small desk with objects placed carefully upon it and a photo on the wall above the desk. It raised my curiosity as it was so promenade in the darkened space. Following my leader burdened with plastic bags I glanced then stared at what I found. It was not at all what I was expecting.

On the wall was a wedding photo. Although showing its age, it was obviously Paul and his wife. They looked so happy, with so much hope emulating from their eyes. Below the photo, on the desk lay a small pure white saucer with two gold rings placed together on it. They shone vibrantly in the gloomy light.

Next to the saucer I viewed a death certificate with a note attached to it. I chanced to stop and read what was written on it.

"To my darling wife. Until we meet again. Your loving husband. Paul."

"You can bring those things in here."

Paul's voice did wake me from a dramatic shock. I didn't wish to be seen to be taking note of the interior so I hurried into the kitchen where Paul was. I was unsure how to relate to Paul after seeing what I just saw. A hurried decision was needed so I decided to be just as it was before, as though I had not seen it.

He thanked me for my help and I assured him it was my pleasure to help him.

"You know the way out?" he said as he started to unravel the plastic bags.

"Yes thanks. I'll see you next time."

"You sure will."

Scott, part 3

The warmth, that only a spring season can bring, had returned. The wattle was still in its glory lining the freeway as I motored along it. I had no passenger on this trip. There was no meter going. The miles can be measured in days on this trip. The load was a machine for which I had no idea excepting the mine I was going to was anxious for its arrival. I was in a truck and I was alone. I needed to be connected to country again. Perchance to find that peace and solitude only the Australian outback can give. Perhaps there I will discover something that I've been looking for. I was still listening to Debussy, pondering upon the mystery, with still many unanswered questions.

I've always found it difficult to stay in the one place for too long. Life is too short to spend too much time looking at four walls. The world is a wondrous place and it is there to be seen. My journey cannot stay still. I have to be always moving, searching. Looking for what for what I did not know. I hoped that I would know it when I found it.

I needed to see different places. I wanted to enjoy the scenery. I got tired of counting houses. I had had enough of being alone between four walls. I was becoming like the passengers, stuck in a time warp, having to be adjusted to the routine of every day similarities. That was not what I was seeking.

Stan, the truckie, the man who was happiest travelling the miles, enjoying the peace of solitude, stuck in my mind. Perhaps

I still had things to sort out and the many miles through this wonderful country may help me in my journey to that mountain of wisdom that I was seeking. Driving long distances gives me time alone in that search for myself and my place into this existence.

I was approaching the town that I had been a taxi driver in only just a few months earlier. The speed sign loomed yet I seemed to be slowing down before it was visible, a course of habit, familiarity. The cars filed past as they did when I had passengers in the car, each performing their routines as a matter of habit. The jacarandas were still in their ugly stage before the bloom in a month's time.

Would I see them in bloom? There was no way of knowing. My journeys are totally unpredictable. I never know now where I may be next week let alone ever. I like it this way. Life's unpredictability is what makes it interesting. I have no home, I have no centre, I have no aims or planned purposes. I am free to be taken where the wind will blow me.

As expected the lights at the intersection of the highway and Lancaster Street were red. This was predictable as they were always red from which ever direction I approached them in a taxi. Why should it be different now? I was with the through traffic, just passing through this town. Yet unlike the other passing through drivers, it was not just another town to me. There were fond memories here.

I looked down each street and had reminisces of each of them. Yet now I see these sights in a different perspective. I imagined all those people in the taxis performing their routine tasks, living their lives as if by habit. Safe in the security that is normality, playing the living game as is expected of them to keep society stable. Gone was their free will.

The highway, the thoroughfare out of this town, was a

forbidden zone for the locals. They were going nowhere.

I saw the old bridge from a different view and noticed the locals using it to avoid the through traffic. The river still remained the only moving object in this town.

The last set of traffic lights before heading up the hill and out of the town. The lights turned green and I noticed the urgency of my other drivers. Pleased to be out of the traffic restrictions of this town. My vehicle was a little slower so I could reflect upon the people I had encountered. I observed many but met no one. They had now become an experience, a learning piece, in my journey to the mountain of wisdom.

The one I wanted to meet I couldn't for reasons that I still didn't understand. The mystery of Chris lingered.

Chris and my paths did cross after the day spent with her repairing the fence. We still enjoyed our chats. I still rejoiced in the vibes that we shared and still felt very attracted to her spirit. I hoped still that something might develop between us. But there was always this veil of mystery. There was a secret that I was not privy to. I wanted to help, I wanted to support her, to be her rock. But I didn't have a key to her walls.

I left her a message on her answering machine and asked her if she would like to go out for dinner, before I left. She didn't reply.

Chris, part 5

I would've liked to have had the opportunity to have talked to Scott for a lot longer. I enjoy his company. He's different to anyone else I've known. He's doing things that I will never get to do. Such a wonderful free spirit that allows him to what he does. Perhaps I'm jealous he's doing what I can't.

He was certainly of help that afternoon. I wouldn't have got that done without his help. I think he fancies me, and perhaps I fancy him. But the circumstances are not conducive.

Mother had text me again before I had reached the house. I wondered what the drama would it be this time. By the time I had reached the house mother was waiting for me.

Ours was a sad house. Not through design but rather from circumstances. My brother, Ken, and I shared a wonderful childhood with our parents. Dad was a successful lawyer in the suburbs of Sydney. We gained our education at the best schools and looked forward to a happy life. I worked as a legal secretary for my Dad, whilst studying law and Ken joined the army.

We were all so proud of Ken when he graduated from Duntroon. Especially Dad, he and Ken were always very close. Dad had hoped Ken and I would take over the family business. Dad was a bit old fashioned like that, but he accepted the Ken wanted to join the army. Although I once heard him suggest that he could learn law through the army.

"Dad's slipped over in the bathroom," Mum said as I approached the house.

Our little house on our thirty acre block had an outdated sixties charm, although it did suit our simple life style. The bathroom was at the back of the house. I hurried down the hallway. There were three bedrooms. Mum and Dad's, mine and Ken's. I passed them all with Ken's being the last.

September eleven came and some bright spark in America decided that there were votes to be won by invading Afghanistan to kill one person. Ken's unit was called upon to join the conflict.

It was early one morning. Mum, Dad and I were still asleep in our Epping house. I didn't hear the knock on the door but Dad did. I did hear Mum wailing. I knew something was wrong. I hurried out of bed and they were in the kitchen. Dad was boiling a kettle for tea. I could see their distress but felt the hesitation from them with my appearance. They were speechless but Dad showed me a document from the department of defence.

Ken had been killed in action. There were no details upon how it occurred but rather words to gratify his bravery and dedication to duty. That was not much good to us. Our family was now destroyed.

Mum insists on keeping Ken's room ready if he might return. She would spend hours in it making sure everything was in its correct place, sometimes just sitting in it. The room, that was always open in case he got home late, was a constant reminder of him to us.

After Ken's death Dad gave up. He could see no reason in persisting. It took all of Mum and my constant support to get him to go to work. His practice declined to the point where by we had to close up the business. We never socialised anymore but kept very much to ourselves. Dad mind was going. We sold our family house and moved to this block in the country. Mum and I hoped the change would help him. It didn't.

I found him lying on the floor of the bathroom. Mum didn't have enough strength to lift him up. Dad didn't rightly know what had happened let alone how to right himself.

We struggled to get him to his feet and seated at the kitchen table.

"Are you right Dad?" I asked when we had done all we could.

"What am I doing?"

"We are about to have tea." Mum said to pacify him.

"Oh," he said vaguely as though he didn't really understand.

"I've got to put Zac away for the night. I won't be long and I'll prepare tea then." I explained.

"Always that damn horse. You are supposed to be looking after us not that horse all the time."

Months have passed. Dad hasn't improved and Mum is becoming very frail.

Scott has moved on. It was to be expected, that's the type that he is. He rang me before he left. He was wondering if we might like to have a meal together. I wanted to go but instead didn't respond to his invitation. It was best that way, I couldn't have gone anyway. Someone had to look after Mum and Dad.

Surprisingly I often think of Scott, I fantasise where he might be now, where his travels have taken him. I travel with him in my imagination for that is as much travelling as what I will ever do.

www.ingramcontent.com/pod-product-compliance
Lightning Source LLC
Chambersburg PA
CBHW030636120726
47904CB00006B/2170